A Game of
War

Season Two

Michael Cairns

Cairns Publishing
Amersham, Buckinghamshire

Cairns Publishing
Amersham, Buckinghamshire
http://cairnswrites.com

Publisher's Note: This is a work of fiction. Names, characters,
places, and incidents are a product of the author's imagination.
Locales and public names are sometimes used for atmospheric
purposes. Any resemblance to actual people, living or dead, or
to businesses, companies, events, institutions, or locales is
completely coincidental.

Book Layout & Design ©2013 - BookDesignTemplates.com

A Game of War Season Two/ Michael Cairns. -- 1st ed.
ISBN 978-1-909699-15-1

For Howard

Foreword

A Game Of War began as a short story, an image in my head of people striding across a deserted, desert world. I can't quite believe how far Ally and Stem have come since then, but I've enjoyed every minute.

What I can't help wondering, is how much further they have to go...

A Game of War
Book Four

Breathing in Space

Intro

The warning light had been flashing for a couple of hours. Each time she came back to herself, it was that much harder to breathe. Stem was in the pilot seat, head resting to one side, eyes half-closed.

They were drifting, breathing vapours. Close to death, and still so far from earth. Would she feel it, the point when her body gave up, or would she just stay on the spiritual plane forever, searching?

She closed her eyes and slipped free of her body, and the Vale. The stars glittered around her and she forgot the fear and the heaviness in her chest. Life lapped at her like waves striking a beach, a universe of souls vibrating and being. But they were too far away!

It was like the beach just kept getting bigger, the sea forever out of reach. She picked a new direction, traveling miles in seconds, only to be met by the same quiet murmur.

She came back to herself and glanced one more at Stem. His mouth hung open, his eyes closed.

"Stem? STEM."

She pushed herself up from the cot, then sunk back, gasping and coughing. Her mind was drifting and she found herself out of her body again, looking down at her pale, skinny form. Her hair was limp, her braids fraying.

She rushed from the ship.

Chapter 1

She was frantic. For three days she had been searching, heading out in spirit form in different directions to find some sign of life.

They had been heading for a station, a place Stem knew about. He had only a rough idea of the co-ordinates, but with their new-found abilities, that should have been enough. Turned out it wasn't. Or the station had moved, it didn't matter now.

She remembered how it felt, on the Homeship and the Nexus, when she'd lifted free of her body, and felt the universe, breathing around her as she accessed the spirit plane. From a life of slavery, to becoming something so much more. Yet here they were, no oxygen, and no hope.

There had to be a better way. Rushing around on the spirit plane wasn't working. There was too much space and she could spend the rest of her life here and still see only a fraction of it. She was still thinking physically, and perhaps that was the problem.

She shouted in her mind, a scream of frustration that was almost tangible. She felt it fly from her, hurtling in all directions. Yes! She screamed again, then fell quiet, listening, opening her mind.

The silence enveloped her, the muttering suddenly absent in the wake of her distress. Then she heard it. A faint response, a response that was growing louder every second. She found the source, and rushed back to her body.

"Stem, Stem, wake up."

She was shaking him, pausing to cough, then shaking him some more. He opened bleary eyes and joined her in coughing, then stopped himself, holding his hand over his mouth as his body shook.

"Stop, stop coughing. Too much air."

"I know where we can go, c'mon."

His eyes lit up and he struggled to sit. She sat in his chair and floated free again, checking the direction, then came back and gave him the bearing. The Vale moved, twisting around, then jumping forward as he half-fell onto the sticks.

She stayed on the spiritual plane, listening again for the sound, her heart racing as it grew louder and louder.

"This is station Nephal, are you in distress?"

"Yes, yes, we are, where are you?"

"Just follow me back, you are not far."

She came back out, gasping in the stale air, but waved at Stem, a smile splitting her face. He gunned the engines, dragging every last bit of power from her, and they surged forward. Within a few minutes the station came in sight, a huge orb from which spokes thrust out into space, ships of all types moored to them. Steel ropes held the ships tight, glittering in the light from the nearest star. The sight of it brought tears to her eyes and she leaned forward, coughing again as she laid a hand on his arm. He turned to her, smiling, then back to the screens, bringing the Vale in to dock.

They waited, feet tapping and fingers drumming, as a docking door crawled slowly out from the spoke and settled with a thud against their hull. Moments later, a loud hiss declared that pressurisation was complete and she hit the door release, gasping in pleasure as cool, oxygen-rich air came rushing in. They sat, staring at one another as they took long draughts, the energy slowly returning to their limbs. Then, as one, they stood and climbed carefully out of the Vale and onto the station.

It couldn't have been more different from the Homeship, or the Nexus for that matter. Bare steel struts ran down the walls and ceiling, the floor a steel mesh that was frayed and ripped in places. She could see patching, sheets of metal overlaying one another, done with a carelessness Dad would never have allowed her to get away with. The vacuum that lay just beyond the thin walls seemed suddenly very close, in a way she'd never felt before.

The voice returned, soft and thoughtful.

"Humans! Welcome to Station Nephal. I am Nephal and would like to make you most welcome to my home. Please, look around, make yourselves comfortable."

She glanced over at Stem, unsure that he had heard the voice, but he nodded at her, then waved at the station around them.

"I'm not sure about the place, but she seems nice."

Laughing at just how similar their thoughts were, she put her arm in his and strolled down the corridor.

The spoke brought them out into a wide hallway that stretched away on either side, wrapping around the entire station. The walls were curved gently, but the sense she had was of standing in a street. The outer walls were covered in gigantic windows, beyond which the spokes thrust outward, like fingers pointing to the stars.

The inner wall curved more sharply, but was still massive, forming the bulk of the sphere. It was covered in shelves, all manner of tools and equipment scattered across them, but further along, the shelves were replaced with booths selling food, supplies, air, equipment, and to Ally's surprise, sex. The two women, wearing next to nothing, stared frankly at both her and Stem, calling out prices as they passed.

Ally turned bright red, and looked away. The further they walked, the more she realised the extent of the inner sphere. It formed the hub of the station, and every thing that happened here, centred around it.

The other occupants of the station were as varied as those they'd seen on the Nexus, There, they'd been surrounded by warriors, strong and proud, but there was none of that here. Here, the people seemed lost, standing around, talking desultorily, and they moved quickly, sharply, as though expecting something to go wrong at any moment. It made her equally nervous, and she glanced around as they wandered, checking over her shoulder.

They approached one of the doors set in the hub, and entered a room, square-shaped, and covered, floor to ceiling, in engine parts. A creature, vaguely human in shape, but with extra arms and stubby legs, came around one of the piles, tools held in two of his hands.

"Help you?"

She shrugged, looking at Stem, then said.

"Actually, we need air for our LS."

He nodded, the finger on one of his hands tapping the side of his nose.

"You've come to the right place. You don't wanna get air out there," he waved with the thumb on another hand at the door. "Come outta here, turn left, fourth door down. That's Genner's place, he'll sort you out, decent price n'all."

He nodded, stepping backwards as he did so, disappearing behind the pile. Ally and Stem exchanged glances, and a slight smile, before they shouted their thanks and they left the room. Four doors down, they entered another room, identical in size to the previous, but this time containing nothing but canisters. A person she could only assume was Genner was sat in a huge swivel chair, covered in food wrappers. He himself was almost as big as the chair, belly hanging over his knees and eyes sunken deep into a face bereft of any shape, or bone structure, or nose. He sniffed at them, then rocked his head back in a gesture of welcome.

"Umm, hi, the guy four doors down recommended you. How much is a canister please?"

Genner stared at her for a minute, long enough that she was about to repeat herself, when he sniffed again, and spoke.

"How many d'you want?"

His voice was thin and nasal and as far from what she expected as it could be. Stem hunkered down next to one of the canisters, and he replied for her.

"We'd need twelve of the two thousands, assuming they're full."

She was taken aback for a moment by the tone in his voice. He sounded harsh, and bored, and she stared at him as he straightened up. He returned her gaze, raising his eyebrows ever-so-slightly. Genner was absently chewing on a bar he had retrieved from somewhere about his person, eyes fixed on the ceiling.

"I could do em for twenty creds a can, s'long as you take em all together."

She covered her sudden cough, then shook her head in disbelief.

"Twenty for each one? We could maybe do fifty for the lot, but twenty a can?"

She turned to Stem, still shaking her head. He rounded on Genner, scowling.

"Your friend said you would give us a good deal, but that's just—"

Genner cut him off, one hand waving the half-eaten bar at them.

"I know who you are. Don't care much, but I've 'eard about you. Things are a little different here, humans."

He nearly spat out the last word, lip turning up into a sneer.

"You may 'ave been special back on your 'omeship, but 'ere you're just another customer, and stuff costs."

She sighed. He was right, she had to admit, even though doing so smarted. Without the air, though, they were stranded here, and twenty a can probably wasn't that much, not that she had much experience with it. 'Can we pay you in other ways? We're both experienced engineers, maybe we can work for you?'

Genner cocked his head to one side, smiling. 'Well, there's always plenny a that sorta work, particularly with the tournament, but I ain't hiring. Maybe you should go chat to Nep, she'll sort you out.'

He nodded, grinning more broadly. 'Then when you got the cash, you come back and talk ta me. I might even bet on you.'

He turned away, and pushed his chair across the floor, disappearing behind another rack of canisters. Ally sighed and glanced at Stem, who shrugged in return before leading her back out into the crowded corridor. They'd taken a few steps, when she stopped, and put her hand on Stem's arm. 'Did he really say tournament?'

Stem chuckled in the back of his throat. 'You noticed that too?'

Ally shook her head, a feeling of deja-vu creeping up to sit in the back of her mind, and snigger at her. Fighting the feeling of resignation that threatened to stop her in her tracks, she looked up at him. 'Shall we go and talk to Nephal, then?'

A little further around the station, and they found a wide steel door guarded by a tall, thin man. His arms reached nearly to the floor, and each one held a gun. As they approached, he nodded, and stepped to one side, pulling the heavy door open on slow hinges. They nodded in response and stepped through the door and into a dimly lit room. On the far side was a floor-to-ceiling screen, white and featureless. Into the silence of the room came the voice that had guided them in.

"Welcome to my station, defeaters of the Atrile. It is a pleasure to have you on board, and can I be the first to offer you my congratulations in escaping from those bastards."

Ally jumped. How did she know about them? She was about to ask, when a feeling of warmth flowed through her, starting at her head and sweeping through her body, until she wanted nothing more than to curl up and go to sleep. Then it was gone, and she found herself smiling, watching the screen as it flashed in time with the words.

"Thank you, that's really nice of you, really."

She paused, then went on in a rush.

"So we spoke to someone who said you might be able to help us. We need to buy oxygen, but we're almost out of money.' She took a deep breath, looking at Stem before continuing. 'He mentioned something about a tournament?'

Her voice was warm, soothing, when she replied.

"That would be splendid, really. Let me explain how it works and we can slot you in. I'm sure there will be plenty of people here wanting to compete against you."

She put out a hand, grabbing Stem's arm. 'Hang on, please, I'm not sure we want to take part, or anything. Could you maybe just tell us a bit about it first?'

Nephal laughed. 'Of course, but please, don't worry, there's nothing sinister about it.'

Ally found herself nodding, believing the disembodied voice even before the explanation.

'It's simple, really. We'll load you up with a light cannon, and you'll fight another ship. Score a direct hit on an engine or cockpit, and you win. You'll win the prize money, which comes from the betting. Following your success on the Nexus, I'm sure we'll be able to find you an opponent, and the betting will be fierce, so plenty of money. Sound OK?'

They agreed before either had a chance to think too hard about it, but as Nephal said, it was simple, really.

The search for an opponent was even quicker than Nephal had predicted, and only a few hours later they were pulling away from the dock, one precious can of air slotted into the life support, and cannon warming up. The light cannon was strapped to the front nose, and wired into Stem's firing module.

As the name suggested, the cannon fired a burst of intense light, a neon signature that would paint bright patterns across the enemy's hull. It was a lovely change from using real ammo, and she couldn't wait to see it splashed across their opponent's engines. It was limited, the battery charged to allow you five shots, although she was sure they would only need one.

As they drifted back into open space, their opponent pulled away from another of the spokes. The ship was tiny, not much more than a cockpit and guns, and painted black. It would be fast and manoeuvrable, a challenge. Nephal's voice spoke softly inside their heads.

"The audience is waiting, begin!"

It was a strange sensation, knowing that your opponent could only fire five times, that every shot had to count. Where she might before have sent the Vale charging off, she could hover, watching the other craft and waiting for him to make the first move. It didn't take long.

Without warning, the tiny ship moved, hurtling beneath the station, then coming back out heading straight for them and firing. With a yelp, she hauled on the sticks, and sent the Vale tumbling sideways. The shot barely missed them, and she was heading back toward the station. Shoving on the sticks again, she pointed the nose down and dived beneath the spokes. Their opponent had vanished, heading off into space and inviting them to give chase.

She turned in her chair, "What do you think?

Stem rocked his head from side to side. "I think we wait. Why go chasing off when he's got to come back here anyway?"

She nodded, but her fingers were twitching on the sticks, eager for action. She reached out her mind and touched him, and just as he had every time since they left the Nexus, he shied back, his mind slipping away from hers. She bit her lip, swallowing the angry words that bubbled up, trying to remember what he had said about it, about how it had felt when the Atrile took him.

"Stem, we need to link, I mean, if we're gonna win this."

"Why?" His voice was harsh. It mellowed as he went on. "We're good at this Ally, we can win without, you know..."

She shook her head. "I don't think we can. These guys are gonna be good, or they wouldn't be taking us on. If we don't link—"

"MOVE!"

She acted on instinct, yanking the Vale out of the path of the second shot, almost feeling it scrape against their wing. The tiny ship was coming straight at them and she slammed on the power, leaping away from the station and out into open space.

The chase was on, Ally twisting and turning the ship as their opponent tried to close them down. He wouldn't fire again until he was sure, and she was making it very difficult for him to get a lock, but he was sticking to them, better than any of the humans they had faced. She relaxed, her subconscious mind taking over and sending the Vale through shapes she hadn't known were possible. Still, he was just behind them, each turn bringing him a little bit closer.

She tried once more to link with Stem, but once more he recoiled. She thumped back into her body, teeth clenched together as the ship rolled and heaved.

"Just, just give me a bit, please."

He shook his head obstinately, and she growled, then reached out, sinking into him. The emotions were still strong, but this time fear washed over her. She tried to calm it, but he wasn't interested, didn't want to face it and conquer it. Their opponent was gaining, matching every move she made, but making it slightly quicker, making every turn slightly tighter. Without thinking, she reached into Stem and pushed through the barrier, finding his mind and joining it with hers. Somewhere beneath, she could hear a cry, but it was weak and faded as she sucked on the power she needed.

Everything got faster, and smoother. It wasn't like before, there was no joy, but her body moved like clockwork, and the tiny ship began to miss turns, unable to keep up. With a flick of the sticks, she turned the Vale upright, stopping it with the thrusters so it hung, nose up and still. The other craft flew past, trying to turn as it was almost directly beneath them, and almost succeeding. The two ships passed within a few feet of one another, the tiny ship scraping past below. She used the thruster to travel backwards, dropping as the other ship flew up and in front of them.

She didn't know whether it was she or Stem who pressed the trigger, but seconds later a burst of white light painted the rear engine of the other player, and she whooped, punching the air. As she relaxed, the link between them severed and she turned to him, smile wide on her face.

As she saw his expression, her grin faded, her hands going to her own, as if to shield herself from his eyes. She remembered the look, it was the same as when he had emerged from the game on the Nexus, when the Atrile had been torturing him. She reached out a hand, but he spun the chair, fixing his eyes on the controls in front of him.

"Stem, I..."

She had no words, nothing that would, or could, make it better. What she had done was sinking in, and her stomach flipped over, her gorge rising. She undid the clips, yanking one hand free of the straps when it didn't fall away, and staggered into the cabin, one hand over her mouth. She had one hand on the frame, her head down as she took deep breaths and tried not to vomit. Slowly, her head cleared and she turned back to stare at him. He was still seated, eyes fixed on the panel, and she watched him, her eyes prickling.

Then another voice spoke up, small but becoming larger, telling her that he should be over it by now.

They had spent close to a week in the Nexus, recovering, and he'd had all that time to rediscover the joy they had shared. But instead, he had hidden away, refusing to even try. Even once they had left, he hadn't spoken of it. Could he really blame her if she just tried to get him through it, use a bit of tough love?

She sat down hard in her flight seat, pressing each control with a little too much force, keeping her eyes fixed on the controls. Then she hauled the Vale around and headed back to the station. They docked, and she got out first, stepping into the corridor to be greeted by their opponent, a tall man with a huge mane of ginger hair and features that looked like someone had pushed them in until his face was almost flat. He gave her a grin, and held out a hand, which she shook with surprise.

"Great game, really. I thought I had you and then..."

He spread his hands and shrugged. She blushed and shrugged back. "Yeah, we, ah, we took a while to warm up. Thanks."

"It's a pleasure. Well, not so much the losing, but the playing was good."

He nodded, and walked away, and she stood alone in the corridor, reeling. She was waiting for Stem to disembark, but five minutes later she was still standing there, and tensing her shoulders, stomped away.

After walking through the watchers, who slapped her on the back, or shouted their appreciation across the crowded corridor, she fetched up at Nephal's screen, mind still awhirl. As it lit up, she was acutely aware of the empty space at her side.

"Ally, welcome back, and well done! What a great game, you must be very pleased with yourself."

The silence hung there as she struggled to find the necessary platitudes, whilst her stomach churned. She glanced around, checking there was no one in there with her, then it burst out. "Actually, I feel horrible, just..."

She trailed off. Did she feel horrible? Actually, right now she felt just fine. A little frustrated maybe, but nothing a chat wouldn't cure. She took a deep breath.

"I'm sorry, it's just that the tournament wasn't great for us, I mean, me and Stem."

"Do you want to tell me why?"

She did. She wanted to talk to someone other than Stem, who'd spent every second since the game back in the Nexus living in some kind of cloud. Bridyant already seemed like a distant memory, and she missed her acutely, like she'd found someone that mattered and then just like that, she was gone.

She stared at the pale screen, but the words wouldn't come, and she shook her head slowly.

"No, thanks anyway. Think I should go talk to him first."

"Of course, well, you know where to find me. The gentleman at the door will give you your winnings. Well done again, really. Perhaps you will play again, once you have had your chat?"

"Uh, yeah, I think so. We're gonna need more than we got for this one, so, yeah. Ok, well, seeya."

She pushed back out the door, craving his arms but not having a clue where to start. She almost barged straight past the doorman, who stopped her with an outstretched arm and handed her the credits. As she shoved them in her pocket, she sighed. It felt nice, having someone like Nephal, who wanted to listen. She smiled, but as she stepped out into the corridor, the money in her pocket seemed to gain in weight, growing heavy, dragging at her. She sniffed, scratching her head, and stalked down the hallway.

Chapter 2

He was gone when she woke up, and she hated that it was a relief. They hadn't spoken when she got back, he'd just climbed into his flight seat and gone to sleep, leaving her the anxious luxury of the bunk. Now the ship felt empty and cold and her neck hurt from where she'd fallen asleep with one eye on the cockpit, hoping that he'd come in to the cabin. She sat up, scrubbing the sleep from her eyes and wondering what happened next.

She was sleeping, and he was pleased that he could sneak out unseen. He still couldn't believe she'd done it. Just thinking about it made the sweat break out on his neck, and he shivered as he tramped down the spoke towards the main hall. What was worse was that she hadn't even apologised, couldn't even say sorry though she knew how bad it was. He realised his fists were clenched and made them open, stretching them as wide as he could.

This place was dodgy. He'd thought so on the way out and felt it even more now. It wasn't anything obvious, but everyone walked around with one hand on their gun, metaphorically speaking. There was a clear divide, once you knew what to look for. The visitors and the live-ins, like the two they'd met when they first arrived. They worked for Nephal, there was no doubt of that, and no matter how they spoke of doing deals and helping you out, the money they charged was going straight back to her. The whole tournament was a scam, one big circle of money, and even the bookie was in on it. He paused at the entrance to the hall, leaning against the corner and watching the world go by.

One of the crew, clothes the same drab greens and greys of the other live-ins, sidled up to him, a smile that made him eminently punchable, smeared across his face. Stem gave him a stare, confident that there wouldn't be anything he had to say that was worth hearing.

"So 'ow long you staying then?"

He continued to stare, but either the man was too thick to read it, or chose to ignore it and had a good poker face. Eventually he sighed and gave way, just slightly.

"As soon as we can refill the LS, we're out of here."

"Ahhhhh."

The man tapped his nose, nodding as if Stem had just let him in on some big secret. Then he dropped his smile, becoming suddenly furtive, taking quick, surreptitious glances up and down the hall.

"You don't wanna stay 'ere too long. Weren't me that told ya, but trust me, get out when ya can."

Only partially surprised, though more perhaps by the source than the information, he lowered his head, speaking quietly.

"Why? What's going on here?"

The man shook his head sharply, more furtive glances that couldn't do much more to make him look suspicious.

"Check out Spoke Four."

With his last mutter, he was off, ingratiating smile painted on once more. With a slight shiver, Stem turned, and stopped abruptly. The sight of her made it hard to draw in air, but now it was tinged with something, a heaviness that made him tired, and his heart ache. His eyes dropped, waiting, hoping that she would say something.

"Stem, I'm sorry, really, I don't, I don't know how to make it right."

He wanted so badly to keep his voice calm, but he could hear the wobble in it, the restrained emotion that made him want to scream at her.

"What you did to me was beyond harsh. Thank you for the apology, it makes it better, but it doesn't make it right."

He looked up at her and saw the tear that was trickling slowly down her cheek. He reached out, rubbing it gently away with his thumb, and she came forward, arms bent in tight to her chest, to shuffle into his embrace. He wrapped his arms around her, but his head stayed up, eyes scanning the hallway, not yet ready to give it all. She stepped away, staring up at him, and he gave her a wan smile, then he told her what he had heard.

"Nephal is running what exactly?"

She had the tone of voice that meant she didn't agree with him, but didn't want to just say so. He bit the inside of his cheek, then explained, slowly.

"The tournament. All the prize money comes back into the station. All the traders here, the food sellers, and the mechanics and even the hookers, they all work for her."

"So?"

He looked at her, wondering how she could be so smart with some things, and so naive with others.

"So, don't trust her. Everything she says and does is for her own agenda, her own ends."

"Ok, fine, I still don't get why that's such a terrible thing."

"It's just, ahhhh..."

He trailed off, not sure how else he should say it. She put her hand on his arm, nodding at him as she stared up into his eyes.

"I get it, really. Don't trust anyone, I get it."

He stared back at her, opened his mouth to speak. But instead he nodded, swallowing the words to sit like lead in his stomach. He turned away, surveying the hall again. She came up next to him, leaning her head on his shoulder.

"So what's the plan?"

Why was he struggling so much with her being so close to him? He shrugged, awkwardly.

"We still need money."

"Yeah, we do. Another win should get us enough..."

She left it hanging. He sighed inwardly.

"Ally, we aren't going to link. I can't do it. Every time we join I remember how it felt, and it drives everything else away until I only have pain and fear. I know you don't understand that, I know for you it's this amazing, wonderful thing, but for me now it's just the worst thing I can imagine."

She stepped in front of him, taking his hands in hers.

"I do understand, honestly I do. But this is me, just me.' She stared up into his eyes. 'Could we just try it, just once? If you tried it and let me help get rid of the fear, wouldn't that be worth it?"

He looked over her head, taking a deep breath, feeling the sweat break out, his neck first hot, then cold and clammy. The station was cold. He hadn't really thought about it, but it was cold here, all the time. He nodded slowly, grudgingly. She beamed at him, wrapping her arms about his waist and despite the chill, he grinned in return.

They split up, she heading back to Nephal to arrange the next match whilst he headed off down the hall, grabbing some unidentifiable meat dish from one of the stalls. He ate as he went, idly wondering where meat came from out here, until he reached the spoke that had the number four signposted above it in crude steel. About half of the spokes, he noticed, were mostly unoccupied, often only one or two ships moored there. Spoke 4 had a barrier across it, a door hung haphazardly in the metal, but he easily found a hole he could look through. The hall was busy though, and he settled for sitting opposite the barrier in a lazy chair that filled the front of a tiny shop selling thick, black liquid in tiny cups.

The taste was bitter, strong enough to make him gag, and he sipped it slowly as he watched the barrier. The day wore on, inhabitants and visitors coming and going. The trader seemed happy to have him sat there, making occasional small talk, soon letting on that she knew exactly who he was. The news of their game on the Nexus had spread far faster than he thought possible, and it made him wonder what the reception would be like when they reached Earth.

He was pulled from his reverie by the screech of the door in the barrier opening inward. The being that stepped out had many arms, and struggled to get over the threshold on his short legs. There was nothing suspicious, furtive, in the way he pulled the door carefully closed and waddled off.

By mid-afternoon, the tournaments had begun and his section of the hallway was quieter. Slipping from the chair, he walked confidently across the hallway, pushed the door, and stepped through. On the other side, the spoke lay in darkness, the huge windows that ran down each side letting in the only light, that of stars. He walked quietly down one side until he came across a pile of tools, some rags, and various pieces of machinery. Looking to his left through the window, he jumped, then scrambled quickly back away from the glass. A lone ship was moored there, with three of the Station's crew swarming all over it.

Sneaking forward, he made a more detailed observation, and confirmed the first thought that had jumped into his head. They were dismantling the craft, slowly stripping pieces from it. As he watched, two of the crew removed the front cannon, fixing it to a trailing rope that came from the entry hatch. Another alien came from within the craft, all four arms laden with devices taken from the control panel. He came into the spoke and placed them on the floor, then grabbed a screened device from where it hung on the wall and tapped various things into it using the plastic-coated keypad. Stem held his breath, hoping the shadows were enough to hide him should the crew-member look up.

The being let the device drop against the wall, and headed back into the ship. Stem crept out again. The ship wasn't new, but it was far from old and he could see no obvious signs of damage. It was a two-manner, and still held some fairly impressive weaponry. There was neat patching on the hull, a sign that the ship was well cared for, so why were they taking it apart?

He eased back into the darkness and made his slow way back to the barrier, checking over his shoulder in case one of them should come inside. Slipping his head through the door, he checked in both directions, then came swiftly out and walked back toward where their ship was moored.

Nephal had been pleased to see her, and keen to chat, and Ally found herself being unusually open and talkative. It would have been strange, but she felt so comfortable there, before the screen, that it simply didn't matter.

Nephal asked about the Nexus and Ally had been relieved to be able to speak about it, her joy coming back as she relived the moments when she had found the spiritual plane and discovered the depth of her power. Being open, not feeling guilty for it, was wonderful, and she realised how guarded she'd been for the past couple of weeks. Nep was a good listener, despite not actually being there, and when she did make a comment, it showed she was really listening, and interested.

She met Stem back at the ship, and they had just enough time to eat something and exchange stories before their next tournament. He was concerned about some of the crew members dismantling a ship, although she struggled to get what was so bad about it. Was he being totally over-the-top suspicious, or was she just too trusting? She was still buzzing from her chat with Nephal, and nodded in all the right places, but it sounded like he was making a far bigger deal out of it than it deserved.

They got onto the Vale and strapped in, drifting out and catching sight of their new opponent. The ship was much closer to their own in design and size, and she reckoned on a fairly even match. The pilot seemed happy to drift, waiting for her to make the first move, so she turned to Stem, eyebrows raised. He hesitated, then nodded slowly and she reached out with her mind. Once again she felt the blanket of fear that lay heavy across his mind, but this time she stayed near the surface, waiting. It slowly eased, and she reached in, letting him come out to find her, his mind touching with hers.

She was hit by a wave of panic and could feel his pulse speed up, his thoughts darting about like flies trapped in a light. Again, she waited, then beneath it all she felt a pulse, like a heartbeat, that felt like love, like they were finding each other for the first time.

She bore down on it, letting everything else fade around her and focusing only on that one feeling. His mind opened and that familiar sense of coming home filled her. Her hands were on the sticks, her body moving as her mind began to sing, and the Vale leapt away from the station, inviting the other ship to give chase.

It came charging after them, catching quickly, then settling into pace behind and trying to find a lock. She took the ship through a series of turns and twists, the station appearing in one screen, then another in quick succession. Their opponent tried to keep up, but struggled, often being left pointing in entirely the wrong direction as they danced and spun. All the time, she could feel Stem's mind, ideas and manoeuvres mixing with hers as they found the best path. She was just lining up to turn completely and take aim, when a voice cut through their joined minds.

"You don't belong here, human. This plane isn't meant for such as you."

The voice was slimy, and brought shivers to her spine. It wasn't the Lords, but it was close enough for a whole swathe of memories to flood in. She faltered for a moment, and the opportunity passed. She realised that Stem was slipping, his mind rushing away from her.

"Stem, come back, what's happening?"

"It's right, I can't, I just..."

Then he was gone, and she slammed back into her body, the sticks suddenly heavy in her hands. She could see Stem, hands held in front of him, eyes staring at nothing, face covered in sweat.

"Damn it!"

She left her body again, letting her unconscious take over, and the Vale jumped forward. Then she heard the alarm as the light cannon splashed a dark red beam across their rear engine. She slammed her hands against the sticks, disengaging the engine and letting her drift. She rounded on Stem, face burning.

"What the hell was that?"

He looked at her, eyes wide and face pale, shaking his head.

"I'm sorry, it just, that voice..."

She gritted her teeth, every muscle in her face held rigid. Her voice was low and barely controlled.

"It was just a voice, just a voice saying things that aren't true. We had it then, I thought we had it."

She stared at the screens, at the stars that spun around them, and clenched her fists. She took a deep breath, then started up and headed back to the station. They docked, and without a word she left the Vale, leaving him in his flight seat, staring into space.

Her face was red as she climbed out and into the spoke, but it was mostly empty. When she reached the hall, she was met with glares from some of the assembled viewers, those that had bet on them. She wanted to know where the voice had come from. Had it been the other pilot? She found her feet taking her at a jog to the spoke he had docked at, and caught him as he was coming into the hall. He gave her a smile, sticking a hand out. She looked down at it, and shook it grudgingly. "Well played."

He shook his head, still smiling. "Not really, I just got lucky."

The voice was nothing like the creepy sound that had caught them out mid-game. She stared at faces in the crowd around them, seeing nothing that made her suspicious, and her face went red again. With a mumbled goodbye, she stomped away down the hall.

Minutes later she was stood in front of the screen, words scrambling over one another to escape. The voice was as soft as ever, comforting and reassuring her.

"Ally, tough luck. I thought you were on your way to winning."

"Yeah, we were, only..."

She paused for a moment, but this time it all came spilling out. She told Nep of the battle in the Nexus, and what had happened to Stem and, more importantly, what he had been like since. The screen was still as she spoke, but when she came to a breathless stop, it lit up straight away.

"It has been a difficult time for you, but perhaps he just needs more time?"

"He's had lots of time, but even so, it was one thing. What about all the amazing stuff we've done, freeing our ship mates, and flying and... It's my world now, my whole world. I can't imagine living without being on the spiritual plane, but he's never gonna want to go there!"

"I understand your frustration, I do, but you must give him time. If you love him, Ally, then it will be worth waiting, and it will be easy..."

"But it isn't easy, it isn't easy at all."

The screen was silent, just long enough for her to reflect on what she had said. She did love him, of course she did, but it wasn't easy. It was so hard, and so wearing.

"Have patience, believe in what you had. I am here if you need to talk again"

She felt a rush of warmth, and smiled. It felt good to have it all out in the open. She should go and talk to Stem, apologise and make things better. She thanked Nep, and promised to return the next day to talk more, then stepped out into the hallway.

Chapter 3

They didn't get to talk that evening. When she returned to the Vale, Stem was gone and she fell asleep long before he returned. The next morning he was crashed out in the flight seat again and she snuck out, her warm and fuzzies of the previous day fled with her dreams, leaving her more confused than ever. She wandered aimlessly around the station, but found herself standing before Nephal's door. She was about to go in, when a thought struck her.

She found a quiet spot and hunkered down on the floor, leaning back against one of the window frames. She lifted free of her body and began to explore. She noticed immediately that the people who lived here had dull spirits, the normal white glow only a sullen grey, as if the life had been sucked out of them. The visitors were glowing bright though, some showing as much energy as those she had seen on the Nexus. She got in close to one of the crew, examining the strange colour. Reading his emotions, she received only a low grade anxiety, like he was permanently worried, but not bothered enough to change anything. Puzzling on it, she drifted away, and came to the thing she was really interested in.

She approached the central core, feeling butter-flies at the thought of actually seeing the face behind the screen. She went to float through the metal wall, but met with resistance, like a soft material, that gave way for a moment, then pushed back. She tried again, with the same result. Trying to see through it, she met blankness, a screen that denied every attempt she made. There had been nothing like this on the Nexus, and it was annoying. She moved around the entire border, and discovered that it was a sphere, and just as impregnable wher-ever she went. She came back to her body, opening her eyes and letting out a huge sigh.

She walked back to Nep's door and went in, hesitating before the pale screen. She knew what she wanted to ask, but instead, began with something a little safer.

"Nephal, where do you come from?"

The story was simple. She had journeyed from a star far distant, searching for the Nexus. On the way she had been attacked, and ended up on the station, then owned by a creature called Malfic, recuperating. It turned out that Malfic was far from the nicest of people, and finding her weak, had stolen her ship and tried to have her killed. Her body had been all but destroyed, but with the help of some of his crew, she had been saved, and Malfic done away with. He had lived inside an isolation tank, and it was this that had made it possible for her to survive. Her body was gone, organs linked up to life support, but the tank enabled her spirit to be contained. Without it, she said, she would have been lost, spread amongst the stars. It meant she could never leave the central core, except in spirit. The station wasn't just her home, it was her body also.

Ally felt the relief like her snug on the Homeship after the long, post-game walk. She hadn't mentioned it, hadn't given any hint that she had tried to see in, but Nep had told her anyway. They continued to talk, the screen telling her stories of the many wonderful creatures that had visited the station since Nep had made it her home.

Ally tried to get a sense of how long she had been here, but time was never mentioned, only events, and people. She would speak about particular talents, pilots that had traveled the universe and wound up here on layover, playing in the tournament for fun, or simply to top up on cash.

Her voice became low and melodic as she spun her tales and Ally thought she could happily listen for days. But the conversation came around to her as well, and she told Nep about the Homeship and discovering her powers. She also talked about Dad. She hadn't expected to, but somehow it happened, and the more she talked about him, the easier it became.

Remembering him like this, talking about the good things, made her mind clear, and her heart lift. She had no idea how long they talked, but when she emerged, blinking in the bright lights of the hall, she was determined to find Stem and make things better.

She was gone when he woke up. He sat in the flight seat, eyes fixed on the controls. Placing his hands on the sticks, he wished he could just fly, get away from here, away from the voices that never seemed to leave his head. She wouldn't ever get it, however much, or hard she tried. They were there when he went to sleep, burrowing away, teeth gnawing at his thoughts until all that remained were fragments that left him questioning everything he was once sure of. Nothing made sense anymore, and nothing was simple, not since the Nexus. Some days it seemed easier to not get up, not even try to exist in the normal world, but he didn't get that choice.

He lifted his hands before his face, staring at them. The shaking wasn't too bad today, and he wanted to go back to spoke Four, and see if he couldn't clarify what he'd seen the day before. He stood, listening for the muttering, and grinding his teeth as it began, quietly, ever so quietly, deep in his brain. Doing helped, so he almost ran from the Vale, losing himself in the noise of the main hall.

He wandered for a while, looking in some of the shops. He returned to the one they had entered upon first arriving, and delved into the parts that lined the walls. There were all sorts there, all used before, and in a variety of conditions. He wouldn't have expected to find new parts out here, to be fair, so instead he began finding matching sets. Sure enough, after only a few minutes, he discovered most of the pieces of a drive and steering mechanism for the same ship, split into dozens of parts and scattered around the store.

It was enough to convince him that what he had seen yesterday was as he thought. So the question that remained was, who had owned the ship and where were they?

As he left the shop and strolled down the hall, he ran through the options. Maybe they sold it for something else. Perhaps they sold it and decided to stay. Maybe they were here and died from old age, or a fight, or an illness. Maybe they lost it in a bet. There were a heap of things that could have happened, yet none of them seemed quite right. Then again, maybe Ally was right. The voices were still there, so it could just be that he was paranoid, losing what was left of his mind. He wasn't sure anymore, but if he stopped trusting himself, then there really was no point in getting up in the morning. With a stubborn shake of his head, he picked up the pace and headed for the spoke.

More prepared this time, he watched the barrier for a few minutes, then pushed through the door and slipped into the corner, where the shadows were deepest. The tools and parts were still there, though different parts from yesterday. He crept slowly up the edge of the spoke and came to the window. Glancing through it, he tried, and failed, to hold in his surprise, his gasps echoing around the empty corridor. The ship was just a box now, all weapons, plate, scanning devices, everything, scavenged from it. There seemed to be no one working on it, so he snuck closer, impressed despite himself at the speed with which they had stripped it. He had imagined a bunch of pirates, amateurs grabbing what they could, but this was the work of people far more skilled.

Working in the Homeship, he had come across any number of engineers with more talent and ability than him, but there had been only a handful that were able to get this work done in the time they had. He knelt and picked up one of the pieces on the floor. It was in good repair, and had been removed properly. They weren't burning or cutting the parts off, and his admiration grew. Checking the corridor, he slipped through the hatch and into the ship.

The inside was much as he'd imagined it, every surface blank, the instrument panel a series of holes with unfinished steel behind them. There was nothing here, they had taken literally everything. He turned to leave, and froze. The sound of voices came floating in from the corridor, and was getting rapidly louder. With a curse he ducked into the cabin, tiny though it was, and waited, pressed up against one wall.

The voices continued, and were matched by footsteps that stopped as they reached the ship. He heard the clank of metal as the pieces were picked up, then the voices began to fade. He let out a long breath, wiping the sweat from his brow, and stepped out of the cabin, then back into the airlock. As the inner door opened, he tried to crouch, to hide, but he was entirely exposed to the two figures stood before him, grins that were all teeth, plastered across their faces.

"Ello 'uman, fancy finding you 'ere."

The one that had spoken leaned back, three of his hands tucking into his belt, the other one casually brandishing a blaster. His companion was the same race, but all of his hands were crossed in front of him, his sallow face wearing a grim expression. Stem swallowed, wondering just how far their dominance of the station went. If they could be doing this here, then maybe they were running the whole show. It was worth a try though.

"My girlfriend is getting on very well with Nephal, you wouldn't want to jeopardise your relationship with her, would you?"

The two looked at one another, grinning and snorting laughter. The one with the blaster looked back at him, still smiling.

"Think we'll worry 'bout that later, thanks all the same. You might wanna think about your relationship with us."

Stem took a step back, thinking about the spiritual plane, about finding Ally, but even as he considered it, the voices in his head got louder, and his whole body went stiff. His breathing sped up and he opened his mouth, struggling to draw air.

"Aww, lookit 'im, Jons, the poor boy's all scared"

The other laughed, stepping closer, arms dropping as his chest led the way. Stem tried to stand up tall, but it was useless. How could he end up here? In the last month he'd done battle against one of the dominant forces in the universe, and come out, if not singing, then at least on the winning team. Now he was about to be done over by a couple of pirates, albeit highly skilled ones.

He broke, slipping around 'big chest' and getting as far as the pile of tools, before he heard the whine of the blaster as it prepped for a shot. He froze, and the slow hum as the oscillator sped up seemed deafening in the silence of the spoke. In that moment, he was surprised to feel the slightest relief that the voices would finally be quiet. He held his breath.

The sound stopped abruptly, replaced by an idle whirring as the power was disengaged. He let the breath out in a rush, then turned to the two creatures, who were exchanging looks. 'Gun' stepped toward him, head cocked slightly to one side. "There'd be no point in killin ya, can't get ya ship with the girl still 'ere, can we? Besides, what 'ya gonna tell people, what 'ave you actually seen 'ere?"

Stem shook his head. "Nothing, I mean, nothing that really means anything, nothing concrete."

"'Xactly. So 'ere's 'ow it can go. Any time you get to thinking about tellin' someone your thoughts 'bout all this," he gestured to the parts that lay scattered on the floor, "just remember that your precious little girlfriend is on this station, an' we run this place..."

He didn't need to say any more, Stem was already cursing himself, realising just what he'd done by coming here. He had to find her, she was oblivious, and helpless. She wasn't helpless actually, she was far more capable than he was at looking after herself, as he'd proved by coming here. But he didn't fancy her chances against these two, not without warning, not when all it took was a blaster in the back. The sweat that was running down his back had gone cold and he shivered, and nodded emphatically. The two smiled at him, rows of yellowing teeth sending him away down the corridor.

As he reached the barrier, 'gun' shouted after him.

"Word of warnin', my friend. We aren't the only ones 'ere who aren't too keen on ya." a burst of laughter followed it, "just a warnin'."

He stepped through the door, the sound of laughter chasing him out into the hall. Leaving it swinging, he rushed back to the Vale.

He was still in the flight seat when she got back, his eyes wearing that haunted look he'd carried around since the game in the Nexus. His hands were holding tightly onto the armrests and she came around so she could look at his face without twisting her neck. He looked up at her and she shivered. For just a moment, she thought he was gone, that someone else lived inside him now, so foreign, and so lost, was the look on his face. She bent and kissed him, and wrapped her arms around his head, and that was when his arms left the rests and clung to her like he was drowning.

When he finally let go, she stretched, easing her back. His face was wet, but he looked worried, not sad.

"We need to get out of here, Ally. This whole place is one big scam, only it's dangerous as well. We need to get as much air as we can with the money we've got, then we get out of here. We can find another station."

She stared up at the ceiling, forcing herself to think before she spoke.

"Why?"

She stopped, pressing her jaws together deliberately, then relaxing them.

"Why do you think that? And why is it dangerous? Nep would never let anything happen to me."

Stem's eyes widened and he shook his head.

"What has she done to you? Why do you trust her so much, we don't know anything about her."

Ally stopped just short of stamping her foot, but her voice was getting louder and she could feel the heat rising to her face.

"Actually, I know quite a lot about her, we've spent most of the day talking, and quite a lot of yesterday, too."

She said it like a challenge, calling him out even though she knew she sounded petulant, and petty. His brows creased together, his eyes clouding over again. She softened, crouching down so their faces were level.

"Really, Stem, I know her, and she cares about me. I mean, she's really interested." She paused, looking around the cockpit. "I think she's lonely."

Stem rolled his eyes and she almost hit him, but settled for rising and pacing across the cockpit, standing by the cabin entrance and gripping the door frame until her knuckles whitened. His voice was calm and measured, and infuriated her.

"I found a ship, being dismantled, a ship that was perfectly fine. I went back again today and met the guys doing it. They had guns and threatened me, and you, if I told anyone about it. I told them Nephal wouldn't be happy and they weren't bothered, like she knew or som—"

He cut off as she thumped her hand against the door frame then spun around to face him."

"Of course they said that! What did you expect them to say? Think about it, Stem, it couldn't be more obvious."

She threw her arms down in exasperation.

"You ask me what she's done to me? What's happened to you, when did you get so gullible?"

His eyes dropped, staring at his hands, and she realised they were shaking. When he spoke, his voice was soft. 'You know exactly what's happened to me. What I don't understand is when you stopped caring.'

She went cold, eyes wide as he looked up at her, face screwed up. No, that wasn't fair. She cared, just as much as she always had. He just needed to get over it, surely it couldn't be that difficult?

'You have to move on, Stem, you have to let it go, how bad can it be?'

When he laughed, she thought again that someone else was inside him. There was nothing of him in the sound, only bitterness and something else, an edge that made her shiver. He rose from his seat, but she was already walking through the door and out of the ship, storming down the corridor. She could feel his eyes on her back, but she wouldn't turn around, she wouldn't. He should have got over it by now, it had only lasted a few minutes, what had been so bad to make him like this? She hissed as she stepped out into the hall, oblivious to the eyes that saw and followed her as she stalked through the crowds.

Chapter 4

She was staring. She wasn't sure how long she'd been there, in front of the coarse metal barrier, gazing up at the number 4 crafted crudely from pieces of wrought iron. It was embedded in her brain now, as inescapable as the memory of his voice, low and accusing. She'd never seen him like that, never imagined he could be that... desperate, but the ground beneath her felt shaky, her foundations falling away.

With a grunt, she pushed the door open and stepped into the spoke. It was dark and felt disused, oddly creepy, as if something waited within to snare her and send her out into space. She walked slowly, eyes flicking back and forth. As she reached the halfway point, she began to relax. There was nothing here, no ships moored, no evil men doing terrible things.

His face flashed before her again and brought with it questions. If there was nothing here, what had he seen? What was happening in his mind so that he not only created all this, but believed, because of that she had no doubt. He believed every word he was saying to her, and it was that, more than the low temperature, that had her shivering and wrapping her arms around her.

It was peaceful in here at least, the noise of the hall blocked by the barrier. The dark made the stars seem extra-bright and she stood, staring out at the constellations. It was odd being in space and not moving, not flying, but it was lovely getting to just look at it all, and marvel at the sheer size, and majesty. Before the Nexus, she'd had no real idea of what was out there, but now every star she looked at held stories and dreams and images, and it was enough, just for a moment, for her to forget about Stem and what was happening to him.

Then the moment passed, and she turned and walked slowly back to the barrier, heavy heart dragging her shoes across the grating. She stepped out into the hall, and saw a being sat at the lone table in a tiny shop opposite. He was staring intently at her, then seemed to register that she had seen him and got up, walking quickly away. She rushed after him, grabbing his arm and spinning him around. He graced her with a fake smile that made her want to punch him, but she settled for pinning him to the wall instead.

"Why are you following me?"

"Me?"

He looked in both directions, face a picture of innocence, and she almost laughed.

"Can we talk about this somewhere more private?"

He sounded like a bad actor, but she nodded and jumped free of her body. He appeared next to her, his features trimmed just a little, making him considerably more attractive and less annoying. She shook her head, and closed her eyes and morphed until she looked like the fur-covered beast Bridyant had fought in the game. She enjoyed his expression, eyes wide and hands held up, despite their incorporeal forms. She shifted back and folded her arms, waiting.

"Did you see what you expected to, in there?"

She paused. Who was this guy and what did he know?

"Yes, I did. What did you think I would find?"

"Nothing. Far as I know there are about three on this side and three the other, unoccupied. Nep explained it to me once, something to do with the spin, keeping it balanced. It's beyond me, but..."

He spread his hands apart, shrugging as he did. She stared at him, eyes narrowing.

"Why are you here? Why are you talking to me?"

He resumed his look of innocence, casually shaking his head.

"You're interesting, that's all. New people on the station, and humans at that."

The 'humans' sounded incredulous, like he couldn't quite believe that she was here, but he grinned an apology at the same time.

"It gets a touch boring here, when we haven't had any new visitors for a while."

"How long have you been here?"

"Me? Oh, years. I like it here, it feels like... home."

She squinted at him. Something still wasn't quite right, and she still didn't trust the way he seemed to change his expression based on what he thought she needed to see.

"You said you wanted to talk somewhere quiet. Why?"

He looked back at her, shifting nervously from foot to foot.

"It's about your fella. Talk's been going round, he seems to annoying some of the people here. Asking the wrong questions, making accusations..."

She was bristling, and, as her control slipped, getting larger until she loomed over him.

"He's been, I mean, we've had a tough time of it recently, before we came here. He's recovering from something and it's just taking time, that's all."

She could hear the doubt in her own voice, and hoped that he couldn't. The look he gave her suggested that maybe he could, but he looked back at the floor, nodding.

"Yeah, sure, of course. You guys looked a little new to all this, just thought you might need a little help, but whatever, you know."

"Hey, thanks, really, thanks for the warning. He doesn't mean anything by it, but I'll talk to him."

She wasn't sure she would though. His paranoia wasn't just annoying her, it was actually affecting others on the station. She hissed through her teeth as she slipped back into her body. The man was already walking away, that furtive look back on his face. She watched him leave, eyes narrowing again.

When she talked to Nep later that day, she found herself asking to play in the tournament again, only this time, it would be alone. Having him on board was a distraction, a reminder of what they should be doing, but weren't. And besides, she was good enough on her own, better maybe, without him there. This time there was someone who had already asked to play against her, someone who had also come here from the Nexus, and seen her in action there.

The usual crowds were milling before the screens as she headed back to the Vale. There were shouts of 'good luck' and fists grasping money waved at her, making it clear it wasn't just her own fortune she was playing for. She still hadn't figured out how she was going to get him off the ship if he was there, but the door was closed and locked, and she let out a long breath, relaxing a little.

Strapping in, she luxuriated in the rumble of the ship beneath her, and the familiar pressure of the sticks. Flicking on the screens, she glanced across to another of the spokes to see her opponent gliding clear of its moorings. The ship was sleek and simple, only two cannon thrusting clear of the nose. Aside from that, every surface was plain, every line geared for speed and manoeuvrability.

She drifted free, all eyes on the other craft, waiting. Then she decided to change her plan, move things up, and turned and fired without warning. She thought for a moment she'd hit him, then the other craft moved, leaping to one side in a way she would have sworn wasn't possible. Her eyes widened and her stomach began to churn. This was a challenge, and the thought of it excited her. This was what she should be doing, not arguing with Stem, or having clandestine meetings with random strangers.

She drifted free of her body, and began the dance, heading the Vale straight toward the other craft. He took a shot and she rolled, diving round and down as the light sped past overhead, then skimmed beneath him, the bellies of the two craft only metres apart. Then she dragged the ship down, taking it between two of the spokes and under the station. He appeared behind her, matching her every move.

She spun the ship, pulling it back up between the spokes and glancing through the windows, watching the spectators step back in alarm. As she came above the station, she stopped the ship, dragging it across to sit above the central core and waiting. Seconds later, the other craft came rushing up between the spokes and passed her, shooting out into space and she fell in behind it, lining up for a shot. He went into a series of twists and turns, and she found herself struggling to keep up, losing all sense of time and place as her unconscious took over.

The station dropped away behind them, as they hurtled into deeper and deeper space. More than once, her opponent completed some crazy manoeuvre that got him back in behind her, and then she was the one being chased. She had no idea how long they had been flying, so lost was she in the dance, in the twist and spin and roll.

He was behind her, and keeping close. She flipped, her stomach jumping into her mouth at the sudden turn, then flew tight over the top of him, staring down at the thin line where his cockpit was. She wished they had met on the Nexus, where she could have got to know him and discover whether he flew like she did. He had to, there was no way he was doing this just in the physical. That thought took her to Stem, and as his face flashed through her mind, that look in his eyes, she lost focus, and that was all it took.

He had come about, catching back on to her tail, and she just had time to glance at her screen when the shot hit. But it wasn't the bright light. She was thrown forward as smoke filled the cockpit, the controls ripped from her hands as the ship went into a spin. She grabbed at the sticks, pulling her hands back in pain as they smashed together. She tried again and succeeded in getting hold of them and tried the thrusters. The fronts were still active and she slowed the spin, though her head was still reeling. She tried for forward motion and got nothing; he'd destroyed the main engine. The screens still worked and she could see the ship hovering, close by, the two cannon protruding from the front suddenly far more threatening than before.

A voice sounded in her head, and she came out again, floating on the spiritual plane as the slimy sound made her gasp.

"I told you you didn't belong here. I warned you, but back you came. Your boyfriend will be dead soon also."

With that, the ship fired. She slammed the side thruster on full and the Vale swung around, just enough for the bolt to career off the nose, taking with it one of her cannon and the tip, including the air sensors. Her mind was rushing with a hundred questions and thoughts, but she had to focus, to find a way out of this. She drifted free of the Vale and into space, then realised what she needed to do.

In a flash she was beside the other ship, sliding in through the smooth metal until she hovered in the cockpit. It was much the same as her own, only this was filled with the spirit of her opponent, a tiny creature not much larger than a child, hands that ended in three-fingered claws and a face only vaguely human. His eyes he shared with the Atrile, multi-faceted and huge and emotionless. The spirit came at her, claws leading the way, but she was ready, the thought of the Vale floating helpless in space making her fists clench and her forehead throb.

She threw up a shield, a clear wall against which her attacker slammed, then stepped back, forehead creased. She reached through the wall, her hand stretching out until it could take hold of the lapels of his flight suit. Bracing herself, her feet flattening until they covered wide circles, she heaved, pulling the creature toward her and smashing him against the barrier. She did it again and again until he went limp in her hands, but she didn't stop, simply dropped the barrier and threw him against the wall. Picking him up again, she pulled them both free of the ship and out into space, where she grew and grew until he was dwarfed by her. Her voice thundered, and he winced as he held up his hands in surrender.

"Who are you? Why are doing this?"

He waved his hands as if he expected mercy, but she continued to shake him, demanding answers. Finally, she stopped, waiting as he recovered.

'A deal, we can make a deal surely. You can have my prize money, I'll play more tournaments, give you that money as well.'

She resumed the shaking, snarling at him, as his head flopped back and forth. Finally, her anger ebbing, she stopped and waited. He gasped, face red, and lowered his eyes, what he had to say coming out in a rush.

"The Atrile, the Atrile, they rule my planet, they rule everything. They told me to follow you, to find a way to kill you. Please, don't kill me!"

She stared at him, eyes wide, wondering just what he thought he'd done to deserve to be left alive.

"Why shouldn't I kill you?"

For a second, his eyes narrowed, and she decided that he wasn't quite as beaten as he was acting. He was almost whispering when he spoke again.

"If you kill me, then there are just two floating coffins out here. I can tow you back, I can!"

His voice rose as he saw the doubt blossom on her face.

"What am I going to do? If I start to run, you'll just come back and get me anyway."

The heat had gone from her face and she could see the logic in his words. Stem would find a way to come and get her, surely, but after she did this tournament, he may not be in a hurry and she didn't have much air left. She shrank down to her normal size and let go of the creature, shoving him away from her.

"You get us back to the station, then we have another conversation. The Atrile might rule your world, but I rule your mind now."

She turned away, hiding her grin. She felt like the guy she'd met earlier on the station, all pithy lines and cliches. She remained on the spiritual plane as she watched his ship draw closer. Wanting to try something, she sent some of her awareness inside his ship, close enough to him to intervene should his hand go for the gun controls. At the same time, she managed to retain some of herself out in space, watching as he moved in close, and dropped a magnet line that clunked against the torn metal on the Vale's nose. Then he turned for the station and engaged the drive, taking the Vale along with him. She dropped back into her enemy's cockpit, nodding. That was a handy trick, and it looked like she might actually get the opportunity to try it again.

The Vale was gone, and as he stood there stunned, he saw again the picture on the big screens, the ships that were in the tournament.

With a curse, he spun around and ran back down the spoke to the hall. Bursting into the noise and bustle, he stared up at the giant picture, then shook his head, swearing some more. Ally was playing, right now, without him. He wanted to storm off, but where to and for what? Instead, he remained fixed to the screens, feeling sick as the camera drones flew madly around trying to keep up with the competitors.

He grew still, along with the rest of the hall, as the game heated up, and the level of skill on display became breathtaking. He knew she was good, but her opponent was very nearly at her standard, and it was like watching a dance, planned and choreographed to the nth degree. The whole crowd gasped as the Vale seemed to stutter slightly, then roared as the shot was fired. When the engines exploded, there was a moment's silence, then the hall erupted into bedlam.

He was already walking, fists clenched as he stormed toward Nephal's screen.

"Did you see what just happened?"

He was dimly aware that he was shouting, but didn't care. He raised his fists, then dropped them, holding them tight against his legs. He stepped back, his breath coming in harsh gasps.

"I thought you checked. You told us you checked that we had no live ammo on board, so what the hell happened?"

The screen was quiet for a second, then flashed to life, the voice contrite and soft.

"I don't know what happened, Stem, I'm sorry. It's a failing on our part and we will rectify it. I'm happy to say that Ally seems to have solved the issue. She is being towed back to port by the other player. As soon as he arrives here we will deal with him, have no doubts about that."

By the time she finished, that quiet voice had entirely disarmed him, and he struggled to find the anger that had been threatening to overflow.

"What about our ship?"

"We will, of course, fix it, it will be as good as new. You will also receive the prize money. I am sorry, truly."

Nephal paused again, and he was left standing, mouth open. He realised that he had nothing to say and closed it, nonplussed. The screen flashed once more.

"How are you? Ally mentioned that you were struggling with the events on the Nexus..."

The voice drifted off and he found himself eager to talk, relieved at finding someone else who was interested in him, who might actually want to know what was wrong instead of just waiting for it to be right. He began to speak, first about the Nexus, then his parents and his life on earth before he came out.

Throughout it all, she listened, asking questions, or just making noises to show that she was focused on his every word. He felt the poison draining from his system, the weeks of feeling impotent and frightened slowly slipping into memory. When he came to a stop, he felt lighter and ready, perhaps, to step back into the world he and Ally had discovered together. The screen flashed into life.

"Stem, how would you like to work for me? I always need good engineers, and you would fit in well here. It's an odd sort of family, but it's a family nonetheless, it might be what you need right now."

Despite her kind words, he suddenly felt his brows coming together, his lips pressing together.

"What do you mean? Ally and I are on our way to earth, surely she's told you?"

"Oh, of course, it's only, with her flying the game alone and mentioning that she didn't think you going to earth was such a good move, I assumed the two of you were maybe..."

Nephal trailed off, clearly embarrassed.

"I'm so sorry, I didn't mean to imply anything, please, ignore me, I was just so touched by your story. You know, there are a lot of people who come here just like you, with no family, no home..."

Her words had faded in his ears. Why would Ally think he shouldn't go to earth? And why wouldn't she discuss it with him? He needed to speak to her, to sort all this out, and find a way back to where they should be.

He turned back to the screen, raising a hand, although he had no idea if she could see him, before turning to walk out.

"Stem, I'm so sorry, really..."

The voice followed him into the hall as he rushed out, his ears roaring with the blood rushing to his head. As he came around the curve toward their spoke, the sound was drowned out by the shouts and chanting of the spectators. As the scene came into view, he was forced to slow, his path blocked. Ally stood, face flushed, in a wide circle made by the crowd. He shoved his way toward her, but succeeded in making it only part of the way. From this new vantage point, he could make out the other occupant of the living arena.

Opposite her stood a tiny creature, maybe four feet high, with an inhuman face, and vicious looking claws. The sight of it, so similar to the Atrile, made him shudder, and try to push back into the crowd, but he was trapped now as everyone surged forward. The chant was growing louder and he realised now what it was.

"TO THE DEATH, TO THE DEATH, TO THE DEATH!"

Chapter 5

The alien slid gently into the dock, the Vale hanging still from the towline. Ally lifted free of his cockpit and dropped back into her body. She used the thrusters to bring the ship next to the dock, where the far stronger magnets took hold and pulled her in. The airlock hissed, and with a sigh of relief, she stepped into the spoke.

She glanced sideways, just in time to see her opponent cross the space between them quicker than she thought possible, claws snapping as it threw itself at her face. Ally twisted and tripped, going down, but she got out the way, and the creature sailed above her. Landing, it spun straight back around and came again. This time, she barely had time to roll before its weight landed across her legs. She felt the sharp bite of a claw into her shin and she shrieked, lashing out and sending the thing flying. Her leg was bleeding, and she watched in shock as it streamed from the deep gash onto the metal grating.

It was coming back, and she was still lying down, still helpless. She pulled her feet up and lashed out, catching one of the claws and sending the creature tumbling. She had a moment to draw breath, and realise she was going about this all wrong.

She lifted free of her body and dived at the thing, dragging it out of the physical and onto the spiritual plane. She sighed with relief as the body sagged to the ground and she faced the being that squirmed and kicked in her hands. The confidence that had left her when the thing attacked came flooding back, and she enlarged her hands until they nearly covered the creature. Its squirming stopped, but it still stared at her with those big, dead eyes, and its voice had lost none of its venom.

"You are being hunted. It doesn't matter what you do to me, they will find you and kill you."

She gritted her teeth and began to squeeze, wanting to close her eyes but not daring. The voice was thinner, panicked.

"I can help you, I know who is hunting you, please."

She had never even considered killing something barehanded, and the feel of it being crushed in her hands made her want to vomit. She stopped squeezing, realising that it didn't have to be done like this. She held him there with her mind, floating paralysed above the grating. Glancing around, she became aware of hundreds of others, the audience from the tournament now on the spiritual plane, watching with keen eyes.

How had they known what was happening? Why hadn't they stopped it? She could see the faces, the eager faces that only a day ago had been peaceful. It seemed that everywhere she went, people loved to see bloodshed, and violence. Well, maybe it would make them think twice if they knew what she was capable of.

She stared at the creature, imagining it becoming smaller and smaller, and it shrank, its spiritual form dwindling beneath her gaze. Within moments, it was no larger than her hand. Once it was half that, she put her hand out and plucked it from the air. With a gesture from her other hand, a small square of steel appeared at her feet and she threw the mouse-sized being onto it. With a lurch of her stomach, and working hard not to close her eyes and scrunch her face up, she stamped on it, feeling it crunch beneath her heel. She stepped away, swallowing hard at the mess that lay before her on the metal.

She dropped back into her body, and gasped at the sound of the cheering crowds who rushed up to her, clapping her on the back and shouting their congratulations. The body of her attacker was grabbed, and carried off, and everywhere she looked she saw the same faces she had reeled from only moments before, smiling and wide-eyed, and all saying the same things.

"That was incredible"

"How did you do it?"

"I've never seen anything like that!"

She was struggling to breathe, hemmed in, but despite the crush she could feel someone watching her. She turned to see Stem, standing back near the inner wall, eyes fixed on her. She tried to struggle her way through the crowd, pushing people aside until she reached the comparative safety of the wall. She reached out and grabbed his hand and he pulled her next to him. The spectators were still milling around, talking in loud voices about what they had just seen, and Stem dragged her away, down the spoke and into the hub. They found the nearest door that was unlocked and ducked in.

They were in a store, stacked floor to ceiling with boxes. As the door slammed, the noise abated, muted voices providing a background hum. Stem was still staring at her, his face in marked contrast to the people outside.

"What did you do?"

"Well, I pulled him out of his body, then just kind of shrunk him down to, you know, teeny tiny size, then I stomped on him."

Her stomach rolled again as she remembered the feeling of his body crunching beneath her foot. Stem was shaking his head, eyes cast down.

"So what, someone gets in your way now and you just kill them, is that it?"

"That's not fair, he attacked me. And you saw what it was like, they weren't gonna help."

"You could have just walked away."

"Where? Where was I supposed to go, they had me surrounded. Stem, he wasn't gonna give up, I had no choice."

She heard the whining in her voice, but it was true. There hadn't been any pleasure in what she'd done, and if there had been any other way to do it, she'd have taken it. His voice, harsh and hurting, cut through her thoughts.

"I guess that's how it works now. If people don't play the way you want you just get rid of them."

"What do you mean?"

"I had a chat with Nephal."

He paused, looking down. Was he blushing? She tried to look at his face, but he kept staring at the ground as he went on.

"She mentioned about you were planning on going to Earth on your own."

"That's not true! Why would she say that, that's not true."

Now he raised his head, looking directly into her eyes, familiar hurt replacing cold anger.

"It makes sense though, doesn't it? I'm not good enough any more, I can't play the same games as you..."

He trailed off, and made for the door. She stepped in front of it, putting her hand on his arm. She tried to make eye contact, to make him look at her, but his face was turned away.

"Stem, that's just stupid, and you know it."

No response.

"Stem, I love you, c'mon, look at me, please?"

He lifted her hand from his arm gently, then let it drop and pushed past and out the door. She leaned back against the wall, hands twisting together in front of her. Despite her efforts, she couldn't stop the tears that came streaming down her face, as she slid down the wall and sat, hunched up, hands wrapped around her knees.

He left the room, mind empty of everything but a scream he was desperate to let out. He was only halfway across the hall before the gnawing began and he put his hands to his head, wondering just how long he could go on before he exploded, or just dropped down dead. He stopped abruptly, buffeted as people brushed past him, and took some deep breaths.

She was lying, it was clear as day. She'd been far too eager to deny everything, pretend like she hadn't ever said it, and why would Nephal lie? He really thought he could trust the station owner now, but even if he couldn't, what was in it for her? Of the two of them, Ally was clearly a more valuable asset to have around.

He walked on, heading unconsciously for the Vale, but as he stepped into the spoke on which it had been moored, he stopped in his tracks. They were there, the stubby guys that had threatened him before, and some others. They had gained access to the Vale and were just climbing in. Before he knew what he was doing he went rushing toward them, shouting.

"Hey, what the hell's going on?"

One of the four armed mechanics, the one that had held the gun previously, he thought, turned to him, waving his hands in a gesture to relax.

"Ello mate, 'ow nice to see you under better circumstances."

"What do you mean? What are you doing?"

"The boss said we was to fix this 'ere ship. Took a pounding in that tournament, ay?"

He hesitated for a moment, Ally's warnings about his paranoia coming flooding back.

"Where's all your stuff? How are you supposed to fix it?"

The man chuckled, slapping his stomach with all four hands.

"We ain't fixing it now, just 'avin a look at what's up wiv it. We'll be back a little later to get the job done, just need the right tools."

His smile slipped slightly as he talked, and Stem glanced around, acutely aware that the spoke was empty, but for him and the five people stood around and in his ship. The others emerged from within, not even sparing him a glance. One, a spare creature with tiny eyes and charcoal skin, was nodding happily as he reported to 'Gun'.

"Yeah, it's all standard fixings, we'll have her stripped in a day, tops."

Stem froze, the figures first looking awkward, then looking at him. The one that had just spoken seemed only then to realise he was there. He caught Stem's gaze, and gave him a half smile, as if to say 'oops, well, what ya gonna do?" 'Gun' gave him the same smile, then an apologetic shrug.

"Sorry fella, looks like things 'ave changed."

He spun on his heel and began to run, then something hit him in the back, hard enough to knock him down. He went sprawling and within moments, there were three of them pinning him to the floor. He struggled, kicking out, trying frantically to free his arms, but they were too heavy, and too strong. He was rolled over to see 'Gun' staring down at him, that smile back in place.

"It's a shame, I think she 'oped you might become one of us, but it don't seem like that's gonna 'appen now. Ahh well, sweet dreams."

His voice carried no regret, and Stem barely had time to register the wrench as it crashed across his forehead and the world disappeared.

She didn't know how long she sat there, but the voices outside had quieted, the thrill of the fight long since departed from the hall as she stepped out of the store room. She needed to speak to Nep, to find out why she had said what she had to Stem. Why would she do that? Surely she knew how he would react? She walked faster, rushing now to the screen and the woman who lay behind it. She brushed past the guard, barely registering his presence and was speaking almost before she entered the room.

"What did you do? Why did you tell Stem I was going to Earth on my own?"

The screen was pale, unmoving, and she found herself staring at it, tapping her foot with her hands planted on her hips.

"Talk to me."

It flashed, and the voice spoke.

"Ally, perhaps it is time that we met, face to face. Please, come in."

The screen slowly swung open and she stepped through, her anger forgotten for a moment as her curiosity got the better of her.

Outro

He came to, head thumping, with the feel of the hard floor beneath his back, and the cold air on his naked feet. He was lying flat, and struggled to sit up, the skin on his head pulling painfully as he pushed himself to sitting. He was in a cockpit, but the controls were gone, only holes and bare surfaces left. He staggered to his feet, skin going cold as he heard a faint thunk, and he grabbed hold of the flight seat.

There was one screen left, showing the front tip of the ship and space beyond it. The craft he was on was spinning slowly, and as he watched, the station came into view, drifting slowly away. He dropped to his knees, hands still clutching the back of the seat. He wasn't on a ship, he was in a coffin, floating slowly out into space.

The inner core was dominated by a huge seat, in which sat Nephal. The first thing Ally realised was that she was human, or at least, entirely human looking; old, with fine grey hair that hung down to the floor and dark brown eyes. The second thing she saw was that she wasn't alone. The walls were covered in tanks, huge, glass-fronted tanks in which hung people, immobile and submersed in a pale liquid. As she stepped further into the room, one by one they raised their heads, eyes snapping open to stare at her.

"Ally, welcome. Welcome to my collection, my talents."

The voice was no longer warm, and what she had mistaken for compassion she realised now was condescension. Nep waved with one arm at a tank farthest from the door, empty but for the liquid.

"Are you ready to take your place amongst them?"

A Game of War
Book Five

Escape

Intro

It was as though the last week had never happened. His eyes were dry and every breath he took left him gasping.

It was cold, deathly cold, and his mind wandered, drifting back over the months that had brought him here. How far they'd come. So much had changed, but it meant nothing now. He'd die leaving her angry and hating him and there was nothing he could do to change it. If he could just speak to her, just for a moment, and tell her how stupid he'd been, and how afraid.

His fists were clenched, barely hard enough for his fingers to come together. The screen showed only stars. Without power, all he could do was lie here - the cold of the steel floor burning through his clothes - and shiver and wait for the end.

A thought, unbidden and unwelcome, crawled up and made itself known. He shoved it down, but it returned, louder and insistent. Fear was the only thing keeping him here. If he just left his body behind, he could search. He didn't have long, but there was a chance, however slim.

He thought of his parents, of what he'd sworn years ago, and closed his eyes. He began to shake, first his hands, then the rest of him, a shivering that became uncontrollable, his entire body convulsing. Sweat poured down his forehead, pooling in the small of his back, prickling along his arms.

He was going to die, why was it so difficult? The steel beneath became the giving hardness of the arena floor, and he could feel again the claws, digging into him, tearing him free. He whimpered, his teeth chewing at his lower lip. A tear, hot, ran down the side of his face, mixing with the sweat at his hairline.

He was going to die. He squeezed his eyes closed, and focused.

Chapter 6 - Ally

Ally was remarkably calm about what lay before her. No, not calm, just resigned.

She heard the clang of boots on the metal floor behind her. The bodyguard from the antechamber stepped calmly into the room, one hand on his waist. She sighed, and turned to face Nephal, who smiled at her, wide and not entirely without humour.

"It must gall you to discover that everything you thought true was a lie."

Ally returned the smile, then shook her head. She refused to give this woman the satisfaction, and asked a question of her own.

"Are you human?"

The smile slipped, only slightly, then she nodded, slowly.

"I was. Now, I am more than human, much more than my pathetic beginnings suggest."

"Pathetic beginnings?"

Nephal's smile became one of sympathy.

"Oh, Ally, have you not yet realised? They are called border races for a reason. You know the term, yes? Humans belong in this universe about as much as the dogs they keep for pets. They have no use, they bring no richness, no value or wisdom. They are a blot on the landscape."

"We."

Nephal raised an eyebrow and cocked her head forward.

"I'm sorry?"

"You said they. You should be saying we. You're still human, however much you try and pretend you aren't. It makes me wonder if that's why you hide in here, so you can pretend you're somebody different, somebody who 'adds value'."

She sneered as she said the last two words, her fists clenched, her face heating up. How could she have trusted this woman? Nephal responded with the calm equanimity of someone content in her lies, in her self-deception.

"I have value, just as you do. Only, your value is to me. Now..."

Her tone changed, becoming brisk and business-like. She stepped out of her chair, and toward Ally.

"There is a container here awaiting your presence. It would please me if you got into it yourself, nice and politely, but I fear you may require some assistance."

She was rubbing her hands together as she spoke, and Ally nearly punched her. Instead, she sat down, and drifted free of her body. The first thing she noticed were the spirits of the figures trapped around the room. They were pressed against the fronts of their tanks, staring at her. There was all manner of creatures, some humanoid, others with more arms, legs, eyes, or simply weight than any human she'd ever seen. They were rapt, gripped by the events unfolding in the core, and she wondered again how long they had been there.

She looked at the empty tank and shivered. It was a little bigger than a coffin, maybe three feet deep and five wide, and bare of ornamentation. Hoses hung above it, waiting to fill it with the strange, viscous-looking liquid that kept the others alive. She looked back at Nephal, who had her hands on her hips and was staring at Ally's body that had toppled gently over and lay peacefully on one side. A moment later, the woman's spirit rose free and spun to face her.

"Your gift is a wonder to me. That one so simple, so humble—"

"Just like you, you mean—"

She went on as if Ally hadn't spoken.

"Could carry such power... you do remind me of me in a way, although I fear you lack my vision, my freedom."

"You call this freedom?"

She saw a slight twitch at the corner of Nephal's eye. The jibes about her station were beginning to hit the mark. Without warning, the woman flew at her, a hand pulling a long, jagged-edged knife from her belt. As she neared, she swung it, stopping just short of Ally, the blade hovering inches from her neck. Her teeth were bared and she spat out her words.

"I am freer than ever I was on earth, and ever you will be. There is not room in the world for such as us, but here, I have my own world, here I am the creator and the master."

As Nephal's composure crumbled, Ally's confidence grew. This woman wasn't just evil, she was insane. Ally focused on the dagger, the tip quivering, blurred for how close it was to her eyes. She imagined it softening, becoming hot, and grinned as the tip wilted, then flopped completely. With a shriek, her attacker dropped it to the ground, waving her burnt hand in the air. She turned her eyes to Ally, wide and panicked.

Ally reached out and grabbed her with a hand the size of a person that wrapped around her and began to squeeze. Nephal wriggled, then stopped, staring at Ally. Her eyes flashed, fury and something else, and she screamed, a sound that made Ally wince and clap her hands to her ears, bending over in an effort to block out the searing pain.

The hand vanished, as did Nephal, and Ally lifted her head to see Nephal's physical body come back to life, and shout orders to her bodyguard. The man ran to where Ally lay on the floor, and pressed a knife against her neck. Nephal, smile once more on her face, looked at her. She wouldn't be able to see her, but her harsh tones filled the room.

"That, I think, will be enough of that. You are indeed gifted, more so, perhaps, than I realised. But some gifts are nothing pitted against steel. You may return to your body before I put you in the tank. I should warn you, I have no idea how long you will last if you don't, for travel beyond the liquid is impossible."

She crossed her arms, and stood, waiting. Ally stared at her, and the bodyguard, then swore, copiously, and slid into her body. She sat up and felt his arms go around her, pinning hers against her body and lifting her from the floor. She was small against him, and her kicks had no effect. She was carried over to the tank, and Nephal released the front, letting it swing open. He shoved her in, and the door slammed, catching her fingers where she was gripping onto the outside, doing everything she could to delay the moment.

The clips closed, and she kicked the front glass. It vibrated, making a deep 'thung' sound, but remained solid. The liquid poured from the hoses, covering her. It was surprisingly warm, and felt almost like a shower. It was up to her waist before she began to panic. As it climbed higher, she held her breath, eyes wide and sweat pouring down her face. Her legs could no longer do anything but kick feebly, but her arms were still free and she slammed her open palms against the glass.

The water reached her neck and traveled slowly up. She tipped her head back and took a deep breath, then closed her mouth. She grabbed her nose with one hand, as the water rose yet further. Her entire body jerked and twisted, and she closed her eyes as the liquid swirled up and over them, then closed over her head.

Her breath was running out, and she kicked again, slow movements in the liquid prison. Her eyes flashed with spots as her lungs rebelled, and before she could stop herself, her mouth opened and the liquid rushed in. She screamed, a strange bubbling sound as her lungs filled up, and she waited for the end.

It never came. It didn't feel like breathing, but she was conscious, and alive. Her eyes were still squeezed shut, but now she gingerly opened them, letting the liquid in. It stung a little, and she blinked furiously, tears mixing with the liquid, then it subsided and she stared out from the tank.

Nephal stood before her, an expression of interest on her face. When she spoke, her words came as if from far away, a distant echo.

"You look like you didn't enjoy that very much."

Ally caught the glare on the glass that separated them, and began to struggle, her chest heaving in the confined space. She tired quickly, her limbs aching. When she looked again at Nephal, she managed a shrug, and was rewarded with the crazy woman screwing up her face. Nephal waved a dismissive hand at her.

"We shall wait. Once you have been in there a few days, we'll see whether you feel the same way."

She tossed the words at her like weapons, then turned and stalked back to her chair. Ally stared out over the room, her thoughts spinning in circles. Where was Stem?

She lifted free of her body and pressed her spirit self against the glass, resting there as she looked out. It was a relief to be out of her body, free from the sensation of drowning, but the confinement was worse here, the universe taken away by a sheet of glass. If it was glass, though, she could have traveled through it. She was wondering what it meant when a voice crept quietly into her mind.

"Please, if you would be so kind, take a look to your left."

She glanced across to the tank next to hers, and saw a hugely-fat alien staring at her. His body was at the back of the tank, partially obscured by the liquid, but his spirit looked just the same, and was pressed against the edge of the tank, as close to her as he could get. She raised an eyebrow, then a hand in greeting and he raised his also.

"My name is Atan, and can I say, it's thoroughly lovely to make your acquaintance, despite our less-than-perfect surroundings."

"Umm, yeah, it's nice to meet you. I'm Alicia, Ally."

He nodded, beaming.

"I'm so excited to hear where you've come from. You're the first we've had here for quite some time, and human at that! I spent longer than I care to remember trying to convince the council that there were talents amongst the humans. Typical that the first one I meet decides to imprison me. You aren't, I'm hoping, like our beloved host?"

She shook her head firmly.

"Not a bit."

She paused, almost not wanting to ask, but her curiosity won out.

"Umm, Atan, how long have you been here."

He shrugged, the movement sending his chins into spasm.

"In all honesty, I really cannot say. I lost count after the first fifty or so years."

Chapter 7 - Stem

It came naturally, though he had no idea why. It was as if his mind had been waiting for him to set it free, patient, but eager, and he rushed from the ship, and out into space. He wobbled, struggling to find equilibrium. There was no up or down here, no perspective. How did he move, how did he stay balanced?

He tried to remember what Ally had told him, and focused on his spiritual body, on the space around it. He was part of everything, that was what she said. If he focused on that, it didn't become about moving a physical shape, but about transferring his energy, his life force, from atom to atom. It didn't help much.

"HELP!"

He could shout, his mind sending it in all directions, powered by the weight of his panic. He shouted again, then turned to look at the ship. It was dark, a floating carcass black against the black of space. Only, space wasn't black, not really. The light of millions of stars kept the darkness at bay, and the ship was a silhouette against the backdrop. What was the chance of anyone actually finding him?

The voices came then, and the vastness about him seemed to close in. They were quiet, creeping, no words that he could discern, and they came from within. They were the same voices that had kept him tied to his body since the Nexus, and he rushed back into the ship, for the comfort of the physical.

He snapped back into his body, and all sensation fell away. His vision was closing in, his organs slowing. He was close to death now, and if he stayed in here any longer, there would be no choice to make. He battled in his head, his body too weary to join the fray.

With a cry he ripped free of himself and went out into space, waiting for the voices, his spiritual self shaking and pale. When they came, he dove down and met them, taking every syllable and tasting it. In the end, they were just words, words he didn't understand, words that couldn't harm him, and he was laughing, his joy tumbling out into space. So this was what she had meant, this freedom, this sense of belonging.

The voices hung back now, subdued, and he shouted again, louder now. He set off, flying from the ship. The station had to be near. He had been drifting, for hours, but still can't have gone too far, not without power. He went as far as he thought he could have gone, then came back and headed in the opposite direction.

He felt weak suddenly, his travel slowing, his eyes dimming, and he realised that his physical body was nearly done. When it went, he would fade also, left among the stars. He gritted his teeth, desperation making him scream and shout, and he turned and headed back to the ship. Then a voice, like water in the desert, filled him, and brought tears to his eyes.

"Stem, it is good that we meet again, I had hoped this might happen."

"Bridyant, help."

Even his mental voice sounded breathless to his ears, every syllable a struggle. A light, one amongst the multitude, was getting bigger, and with it the reassuring tones of the alien, telling him it was going to be OK, just to relax, and get back to his body before he was disconnected entirely. He sank back into the stripped-out ship, and into his body. He could feel nothing, no sensation beyond the light, desperate breaths that failed to move his chest.

The light faded, and then even Bridyant's insistent voice was gone.

When he awoke, he got a few blessed moments of relief, before the headache set in, and he rolled to the side of the cot and vomited. Every part of him ached, as if he'd been running, constantly, for days.

The cabin around him was small, cozy and definitely not the carcass upon which he'd been left to die. From his position curled up on his side, he saw two legs, pale, mottled grey, walk past him, then bend and begin to mop up the sick. He squeezed his eyes closed, face burning. He managed to roll onto his back and reopened his eyes, staring at the side of Bridyant's head. She turned and gave him a smile, that slightly scary look that meant she was actually happy, and he gave one back. Had he not been about to die from pain, he'd have leapt from the bunk and kissed her.

That day was blurry and painful, but the next he sat up, and ate something, and managed a conversation, albeit brief. The third day since his narrow escape, he was walking around the tiny ship, checking out the modifications that Bridyant took great pleasure in pointing out. It was later that same day he told the alien about what had taken place, and led him to be floating in a dead ship.

"But, Stem, why were you and Ally arguing, why did it start?"

He shook his head, blushing as he thought about it. It all seemed so petty, so meaningless now.

"She, she was so impatient with me finding the spiritual plane again, with me getting over what happened on the Nexus."

Bridyant looked at him sideways, her eyebrows raised sharply.

"That doesn't sound like Ally. Don't get me wrong, I know she was passionate about her powers, and rightly so, but she loves you, I find it hard to believe that she would be so callous."

He nodded, then a thought struck him.

"I could never find the words to explain what was happening on the station, which is weird because it was pretty blatant. It was like Ally just wasn't interested, like that woman had somehow become more important than me."

"Alicia would never go to Earth without you. And you know that. How could you doubt that, even for a second?"

He shrugged.

"But it..."

He tailed off. It had seemed so simple when they'd been there...

"It was her, wasn't it? Nephal was doing a number on us."

Bridyant raised her hand, palms up, and shrugged.

"I do not know this person, so I cannot say, but it does sound like something external was affecting you."

She leaned closer, making eye contact.

"What happened on the Nexus was terrible, Stem. Alicia was impatient, of that I have no doubt, but she would never have acted as you described, not without something else going on. Might I suggest we pay a visit to this station and find out exactly what has happened to your girl friend?"

He nodded, stood, then slumped back down in the second's chair, head spinning. Bridyant put her hand on his shoulder, smiling slightly.

"Be careful. It has only been three days. Your brain may have survived the oxygen starvation, but your body is still weak. Just relax and I'll find the station. How long were you drifting?"

He could do better than that, the co-ordinates of the place burned into his mind by the fierce relief they'd felt upon arriving. A few hours later and they were floating in space, right where the station had been. There was another hulk, a few miles from the station and they scanned it, Bridyant travelling in spirit. He waited, knuckles white against the sticks until she returned and shook her head. They swapped seats and he thudded down into his, slamming his hand against the armrest.

"Was there anyone on there at all?"

She shook her head.

"So where the hell has it gone?"

Another shake.

"Most big stations have pretty good drives. They don't move because people need to know where to find them, so I do not imagine it has moved too far."

She turned in her seat and looked at him.

"Are you ready to access the spirit plane again?"

He nodded, taking a breath. She grinned at him, then leaned back and closed her eyes. He did the same and moments later, he floated in the cockpit, watching as Bridyant drifted through the wall and out into space. He followed her and they hung, side by side, surrounded by stars.

"How are you feeling?"

"I'm fine. I think whatever was happening on the station was also making me more scared than I needed to be. I mean, it took nearly dying to get me to do it, but, you know, now it's no effort."

She nodded, then motioned in one direction with her head and shot off in the opposite. He watched her go, a vague trail of light streaming out behind her, then sped off. He found as he flew that he could spread his mind out, scanning the space on either side of him. It didn't take long for him to realise the enormity of the task that lay before them. Finding the station in the first place was an incredible stroke of luck, and he and Bridyant could spend the next year and not do the same.

He headed back to the ship, then flew again, on a course perpendicular to his first. His search was just as fruitless, and when they convened on the ship, hours later, his patience was slipping.

"Damn it, Bridyant, we're never going to find it."

He punched the wall and sat down heavily in the chair, hissing air from between his lips and closing his eyes. He rubbed his temples, waiting for the alien to say something that would make it better.

"I think that you are right. We could keep searching, I am happy to, really, but it is a slim hope that we will find anything."

His head sank until his chin rested on his chest. For the first time since Ally had dragged him free of the Lords, he felt utterly helpless, his eyes prickling as he blinked rapidly. He wouldn't cry, not in front of Bridyant, and not until he was sure there was nothing they could do.

"What are our options?"

She nodded, leaning forward.

"She will head for earth, eventually, so we could go there. We could keep searching here. We could fly to the nearest station and ask around, see whether she has passed through, or if anyone there has come from Nephal and knows where it is."

She paused.

"She loves you. Do you not think it strange that she didn't come after you, once you had disappeared?"

The same thought had been rattling around his brain, but he had refused to entertain it. The question made up his mind.

"We can't go to Earth. We have to find Ally. You're right, she would never let me die, which means something has happened to her. How far is it to the nearest station?"

"We can be there in a day, but I think it more sensible to go to a different one. Gateway is two days away, but it lies on the lane that goes past Earth. Most traffic stops there, it is a good place for us to ask questions and not be noticed."

He nodded, and strapped himself in. She laughed, the barking sound he still hadn't got used to, and they shot away.

Chapter 8 - Ally

Atan's eyes were closed, his body sagging at the bottom of the tank. She'd freaked out when he said how long he'd been here, and gone back into her body, kicking and punching the glass in agonising slow-motion. By the time she recovered, he'd left the spirit plane, and now she lay against the front of the glass, in spirit, oblivious to the liquid around her.

Her attempts to contact any of the others had been fruitless. In the first hours, she had imagined it would be the confinement that drove her mad, but now she thought it more likely to be the loneliness. She shouted through the glass, sending her thoughts at the rotund alien, and his eyes flashed open, then found, and settled on her face.

He broke into a smile, then his eyes closed again and he lifted free of his body.

"Ally, splendid! That was a most impressive display. You are strong, young lady, if you are able to reach me through this stuff."

He floated up until his head brushed against the glass at the top, eyes still fixed on her. She had a hundred questions she wanted to ask, and picked one at random.

"How did she get you?"

The alien laughed, shaking his head, then looked down, face reddening slightly.

"I come from a long-lived race. We have been exploring the universe for millennia, always with the aim of learning, of finding new people to share our learning with. Long before I came of age, my people ostensibly ran the universe, or at least contributed to the governing thereof."

He paused, then chuckled.

"I'm sorry, this has very little to do with your question, but it is nice to talk to someone new."

She shook her head, gesticulating.

"No, please, I don't mind. I had no idea about any of this, about how big things were..."

She drifted off, staring around the chamber. He looked at her curiously.

"Perhaps, you could tell me a little of your story as well. I would be intrigued to discover how a human came to be here."

She nodded, forgetting his story for a moment as the last few weeks flashed through her mind. For the second time that week, she told her story. He was attentive, asking question rarely and listening intently. It was a very different experience than speaking to Nephal had been. Where she had sympathised and empathised at every turn, he just listened, head cocked slightly to one side.

When she finished, he nodded.

"I believe your friend, Bridyant, is right. You are special, Ally, quite different from others of your race, and indeed any other race."

He stopped, beaming.

"Splendid!"

She laughed, blushing, and shook her head.

"How can you be so happy, when you're trapped in here?"

"My people discovered, back when everyone else in the universe was still running around hitting one another with sticks, that joy and contentment, could not be found externally. It sounds so simple when said like that, so basic, but this is a fundamental truth, that all recognise, but so few truly understand."

She sifted through his words, finding nothing she didn't already know, but also realising that he was right. She had spent her life pointing at others for her misery, her suffering. First the Lords, then the Master and now Nephal. But it hadn't been personal. It hadn't been about her at all. Still, she had made the choice of how to react, of how to live within the situation, and that was what he was saying. His choice had been to see every situation in a positive way, regardless of his circumstances.

She understood now, but could she do it? He was looking at her, a faint smile on his face, nodding slightly.

"You are definitely special. It is easy for me, for my race also, because in every situation there is the chance to learn, to evolve and become richer than we were before."

He chuckled.

"I admit, I feel like I have sucked the learning dry from this particular environment, but then, look how wrong I was about that, because here you are."

He spread his hands apart, as if her coming was the most wonderful thing in the world, and she couldn't help laughing.

"You were going to tell me how she caught you."

"Ahh, yes, well, ok then, here we go."

"I never get bored of space. I would sit in my cockpit, staring out at it. Stories, Ally, stories. Every flickering light carried with it the lives of millions, billions of beings, each with their own stories, their own things to teach me. It was, I believe, the reason I was chosen as a Seeker.

"It was a proud day, the flags waving over us as we stepped up, were handed our codes, and ship names, and granted access to the central library. I was chosen that day to go out into the universe, to find things and send them home, to broaden our knowledge, and I couldn't have been more thrilled.

Others were worried, scared of leaving home, of leaving behind loved ones. I was gone before night-fall, engines on full, heading into the black.

"Years passed, and I found more than I had hoped, more than I believed possible. New races, and what races they were. I discovered a planet covered in water, the inhabitants evolved from the fish found on most planets, to huge things, the size of a spaceship, with brains to match. They swam the skies in their spiritual form, massive ghostly beings that made space their own.

I met the forest people of Ceylen, a planet on the far reaches of space, destined never to be found, except by one such as me. They have no interest in the rest of the universe, content to roam the forests. They would be considered simple by most, using rudimentary language, a few tools, but their evolution has gone in different directions. There is no war there, no violence. They exist as one people, joined by their minds, almost a hive, I suppose you could say. Joining with them was a revelatory experience. Back home, we were jealous of our privacy, clinging tight to the secrecy of our minds, but you can not join with the Ceylen without relinquishing that. I find it oddly comforting that, should I never leave here, this is a race of people who know my every secret, my life caught in their consciousness."

He paused, and she took a moment to revel in it, in what she was discovering. There was so much. She had seen it on the Nexus, but that had been a fraction, nothing more. He went on, his voice taking on a sing-song tone.

"My people began to shrink. The universe was changing, the elder races no longer afforded the respect they once had, instead replaced with those who could grab the most, and keep hold of it. It was in this time that the Atrile, those monsters you know so well, emerged. They had a similar plan to us, finding those people who have not found the spiritual plane, who have not yet found the world beyond their planet. But while our brief was to explore, and learn, their's was to conquer, and take, and enslave.

"Over time, we vanished, our system no longer open. We became a myth to some, the younger races whose memories contained no trace of us, and others assumed we had died out. The Ceylen had given me an idea, one my race jumped on when I presented it. We have cut ourselves off now, our system shielded from those who come too close, and we live in peace, in isolation. There were some of us though, for whom the lure of space was too great.

"We seekers were given leave to travel still, to observe and send back what we found.

"I found myself drawn to the centre, to the planets that were crowded, people from all over gathering together. The sheer weight of minds was fascinating, and I was incorrigible, desperate for those that were different. Mysteries caught me, held me spell-bound, and I searched for them. Station Nephal was one amongst hundreds, a folk tale of the station that moved, that couldn't be found. Of course, I had to find it.

"She sucked me in with a promise. I had been here a few days when she asked me to meet with her, or at least, her screen. She knew who I was, though I don't to this day know how. She told me she had the most wonderful information, knowledge of which I could only dream, and like a fool, I was sucked in. Even her shield didn't make me uneasy. It was, she said, to keep the information safe, that it was dangerous should the wrong people get it. I still believe there was more at work than my pride and her wily ways, but I have been unable to prove it, stuck as I am.

"Nonetheless, I stepped through the screen when it opened, and a cloth went over my face and I awoke in here."

He sighed, his face suddenly bleak. Then he shook his head and smiled at her.

"I dream of my ship, but I fear it is long gone now. But the stars are still there, and of them, my dreams are constant, whether asleep or waking. I will see them again, I don't doubt."

She was silent, her own life feeling suddenly very small. She had dreams of reaching earth, of having a place to call home, yet here was Atan, who had spent his life away from his, and seemed all the better for it. There was more to her quest than getting home. Still...

"You are optimistic, considering how long you have been in here."

He smiled, one stubby finger coming up to point at her.

"Ahh, but then, I have always known there was something, or someone, who would free me. Perhaps you are that person."

She shrugged, then thumped the glass with one hand.

"I know I won't still be in here in fifty years, or even fifty days."

He nodded, thumping one fist into the other, and making a mock-angry expression with his face, eyebrows scrunched together. It was almost comical, but there was an edge there, something hidden deep beneath his cheerful exterior.

"So, have you spoken to the others?"

She motioned around the room. He nodded.

"They are less sociable than me, and though I was the first here, they have struggled more with the confinement, and the loss of liberty. Were I to be honest, I might describe a few of them as... less than sane. But they are good people, and powerful, every one. Say what you wish of Nephal, she recognises power when she sees it."

They fell silent. Then a voice made her jump, and she span around in the tank. The owner of the voice was in the cabinet the other side of her, free of his body and staring at her. He was more normally shaped than Atan, but still far from human. He had no nose, his mouth set just below his eyes. Above the eyes, his forehead was huge. She knew she was staring, but it was so strange, seeing a face so apparently normal, yet so entirely different. As she recovered from the shock, what he was saying sank in.

"Adventuring is indeed a wonderful way of life, Ally, but it is knowing there is a home to return to that makes it so special. Without the home, it is merely wandering. You can try it, but you will find it a lonely business."

Her mouth hung open.

"How...?"

Atan chuckled, and she spun to face him.

"Lucid, you know that really is terribly rude."

He turned his gaze to her.

"Our friend Lucid here has the handy ability to pick out thoughts. He likes to call it mind-reading, but the truth is he can only pick up what you are thinking at the time, and even then, it is far from accurate."

Ally turned back to the alien, mouth still hanging open.

"Really?"

He nodded, sketching a slow bow.

"I am Lucid, and what Atan says is correct, damn his attention to detail. And you are Ally, and you are here to save us, I hear?"

"Huh? Where did you?"

Lucid had already nodded past her towards Atan and when she turned to him, she saw he wore a guilty smile. He spread his hands before him, batting his eyes.

"I am an optimist, what can I say."

She sighed.

"I cannot guarantee anything, but I do intend to get out of here, and when I do I will certainly take you with me."

A hand slammed against the glass, and she jumped then slid back into her body. Nephal was stood before her tank.

"Wake up, human. You and I need to talk."

Chapter 9 - Stem

It glittered before them, huge and sprawling, and he wondered how he'd missed it on the way out from Earth. It wasn't as big as the Nexus, but it was spread out, long gantries thrusting out like the limbs of a spider. That wasn't right though, because these limbs didn't curl evenly, but jutted in all directions, with kinks and right angles joining them together. It was more like looking down on a maze, but with all paths leading to the centre. The centre was huge, a multi-sided shape that looked a little like someone had made a cube, then beaten it about with a hammer. Smaller parts jutted out, lending the entire thing an air of chaos.

The gantries were covered in ships of all sorts. On the far side he could see a huge, straight gantry, on which were moored three enormous craft, close in size to the Homeship. Bridyant was watching him with a wry smile.

"This is the jumping-off point. Once you get past here, you enter Atrile territory, the outer reaches."

She paused.

"You did well coming out here the first time. There are many experienced pilots who count this as the edge of space, the furthest they will go. I think it was destined that you were to find Alicia."

He winced at her name, then nodded.

"Let's hope that destiny still works. Where are we docking?"

Bridyant pointed to the screen, showing a thicker gantry that ran straight from the station, and was host to a variety of small ships.

"My people are sponsors of the gateway. It allows us certain luxuries, which I do not mind confessing I am grateful for. We dock there, and we do not have to take a walk."

She gestured to one of the thinner spindles that made its crooked way from the station. Stem could see figures, clad in space suits, emerging from their docked ships and pulling themselves toward Gateway via steel ropes. He looked at Bridyant, one eyebrow raised and she smiled in return.

"The life of a pilot is lonely and tough, and oftentimes poor. You can pay for a closer mooring, or even to be on one of the luxury legs, but they have better things to spend their money on."

"Such as?"

Her smile turned sympathetic, then she barked.

"You will see, though it surprises me that you cannot guess."

There was a soft clunk as they latched on, Bridyant's ship sliding into a set of huge mechanical arms, that closed lightly around it. Glancing through the screen one more time, he saw the gantry close up, and was surprised by the number of cracks and bad repairs. When he pointed it out to Bridyant, she laughed again.

"You have had a rather unusual view of things, first on the Homeship and then the Nexus. The rest of the universe is a little less affluent, and more, what would you say, 'hand to mouth'? Gateway is quite well maintained, and enjoys regular custom, but step out of the shipping lanes, and you will see a different story."

She had unstrapped and was attaching pieces of weaponry to her belt and powering down the ship as she spoke.

"The widespread dislike of the Atrile is not just about their subjugation of your race, but also their greed and their wealth. The life they live is rare, as you will soon see."

The hatch hissed as they equalised with the Gateway, then they stepped off the ship and down into the gantry. With the screens gone, the world suddenly shrank to a long corridor, lined with dull steel supports and a silver mesh on the floor. There were others, some climbing back onto ships, others sauntering toward the centre. He and Bridyant joined the flow.

There were fewer surprises this time, the flood of life containing all sorts, but less variety than on the Nexus. Almost everyone was humanoid in shape, the differences less marked and more cosmetic. Back on Earth, he'd seen people he assumed were aliens, extra eyes or strangely-coloured, and it felt much the same here. The gantry was long, and took them fifteen minutes to walk down. He was just beginning to get a sense of the size of the place when they stepped out into the station itself.

The beaten cube he'd seen from outside, seemed to be mostly hollow inside, and the space was breathtaking. Before them, the floor of the station was covered in people, machines, market stalls, and a huge number of stair cases, lifts and escalators. It reminded him of the malls back on Earth, only the roof was so high as to be out of sight, and no planning had gone into where everything was. It was like someone had thrown everything in here, then shaken it up. He realised his mouth was hanging open and closed it quickly.

Looking up, he could see platforms, hundreds of balconies and mezzanines, sticking out from the walls, and in some cases, hanging in mid air. Thousands of lines and cables were hanging down from above, and everywhere he looked he saw lights, tiny bulbs that seemed to float, but were in actuality strung on the thinnest wires. The sound was over-whelming, a wall of noise as thousands of pilots, tourists and crew went about their daily lives.

Bridyant grabbed his hand and set off across the floor. They soon passed through the crowds and into a quieter part of the station. The platforms were lower here, and created a ceiling. Bridyant chose a set of stairs and bounded up them, whilst he struggled to keep up. At the top, they stood on a platform, home to more lifts and escalators, and a small man bearing what looked suspiciously like baked hands on a tray. She choose a lift and they scrambled in, then hurtled upward.

The view was breathtaking, each platform home to a different group of people, or stalls, or shops. Many of them contained bars or restaurants, where people lounged on sofas or sat upright on stools, drinking and talking. Other platforms were covered, huge tent-like canopies hanging over the edges. The floor was visible only through tiny gaps, but as they rose higher, it disappeared completely.

He had expected it to get quieter as they rose, but instead, even more people crowded the lift and the platforms. Bridyant muttered in his ear as he stared through the glass walls of the lift.

"For many who come here, the floor is all they see. For those of us with a little more experience, the higher levels weed out the less pleasant hawk-ers like the 'hand man' down there, and provide a little more comfort. Anyone passing through Nephal is likely to be more knowing in the ways of these things. Also." she said as the doors slid open and they stepped out. "The atmosphere is far nicer."

He stopped his jaw from flapping open again, and stepped to one side, allowing others out of the lift. The platforms below them were covered by huge white canopies, but they were joined, platform to platform. The effect was like standing above the clouds, the world below a white field that bobbed gently in the warm air that rose from below.

The platform on which they stood was huge, stretching all the way down one wall and out to nearly halfway across the station. It was ringed by massive poles, atop which huge round bulbs emitted a gentle white light. There were stalls and stands, manned by quiet servers, and chairs, sofas, rugs, and stools, all manner of tables and cushions, scattered at random.

"It is normal in some places, to talk to strangers, to make connections with people you do not know. I prefer these places, they feel more like home. Come, let us get something to drink and find someone to speak to."

He found himself led between lounging aliens to a pair of sofas near the edge of the platform, inhabited by a reedy looking creature, legs folded beneath him, extraordinarily long nose wiggling as they sat down. He spoke in a strange language, fast and high pitched, and Stem couldn't help but be impressed as Bridyant replied in the same language. Then she turned to him, and in common, asked him to step onto the spiritual plane.

He still had to take a deep breath, but it was becoming easier each time and he was soon floating above his body. The platform seemed suddenly busy, the semi-translucent figures floating here and there, and Stem realised why the place seemed so quiet. The reedy man spoke and he found he could understand him.

"You have just come off-ship. You smell of small spaces and fuel. Where have you come from?"

Stem was taken aback by his bluntness, but judging from Bridyant's response, this was fairly standard.

"The Nexus, originally, but since then, a station called Nephal. Have you been there?"

The man hissed, his nose twisting around as if it were trying to tie itself in a knot.

"I haven't, but I have heard of it. They say it moves, that those who have docked there and escaped can never find it when they go back."

Stem leaned forward.

"Escaped?"

The alien turned to him, shrugging.

"It seems that the owner of the station runs some kind of game, a duel of sorts. Lots of betting, money exchanging hands, not everyone can pay..."

He spread his hands apart, then glanced over his shoulder and down across the station. Then he turned back and shrugged again.

"That's what I heard. But then, I also heard that it's just a myth. You say you have seen it?"

Stem nodded vehemently.

"I've been there. There is a game, but I didn't see anyone getting into trouble over money. Other stuff maybe, but not the betting."

Bridyant stepped back in.

"Have you met anyone in the last few days who says they have been there?"

He shook his head, and she nodded, thanked him for his time and vanished. Stem fell back into his body and had to scramble up to keep up with Bridyant. He drew level with her.

"Is that it? We barely spoke to him."

She looked at him, eyebrows raised.

"The next time someone asks him about Nephal, he can tell of how he met a human who had escaped. He can confirm the existence of something thought by some to be a myth."

He shook his head, still not sure what she was getting at.

"Information, Stem. Information and time, the two greatest assets, the two rarest things in the universe."

She paused, scanning the room.

"And right now, we are short of both."

Then she set off, heading for a booth that was proudly displaying huge spinning cups on poles. The drink they were offered was dark and steaming, and smelled sweet and he found himself suddenly thirsty. Bridyant bought them both a cup and they settled in tall chairs next to the booth. An alien, tall and confident, paused to buy some and Bridyant engaged him in conversation, another language Stem didn't know. He moved on and she shook her head. The day wore on, though the lights never changed, and the crowd around them moved and changed, and everyone they spoke to had the same story to tell.

He was getting desperate, his hands sweaty every time they spoke to someone new. The never-ending daylight in here was making his head hurt, and the constant jumping between planes was wearing him and his patience out. He was slumped on a sofa, his eyes nodding, when he heard the gruff alien they had sat beside say the magic words.

"Uyuh, I just bin there."

He sat up, weariness falling away as he leapt from his body and waited for them to join him. They appeared before him, Bridyant staring intently at the alien. He was fat, a big gut threatening to escape his waist band at any moment, and jowls that hung down past his chin. His hair was long and lank, straggly and deep-orange in colour. He spoke again, his thick accent hard to decipher.

"Yup'n, I spen' the lass few days there, jus' fuelin' up, washin' the games."

Stem could barely wait until he had finished, every drawled syllable lasting forever.

"Where is it?"

"Huh?"

"The station. Where is it?"

The big man shook his head, slowly, and Stem's heart dropped.

"I got the co-ords in ma baby. You wanna come grab 'em?"

He nearly shouted, then was back in his body quicker than he thought possible, pulling at the alien's sleeve to get him out of his seat. The man slowly opened his eyes, squinting at them as they stood, staring impatiently down at him. Then he cleared his throat, a complicated procedure that seemed to take far longer than necessary, and sipped his drink.

"It 'ccurs to me I ain't quite sure whas in this fa me..."

He tailed off, tapping his stubby fingers against the arm of his chair. Stem looked at Bridyant, and she shrugged, then turned to the fat alien.

"I'm not sure that we have much of value, what would you be interested in?"

"Well."

He coughed, hawked something up, then swallowed it down.

"Ahm not all that sure that I need much a any-
thin' right now."

The sweat broke out on Stem's head again, and
he had to grab the arms of the chair to stop from
jumping at the man. This wasn't going how he'd
imagined it.

"There must be something we can give you. What
do you need?"

"You folk seem awful keen on findin' Nephal.
Whas yo int'rest in it, if'n ya don' mind me askin'?"

Bridyant got there a second before Stem.

"We owe her money. We need to get there and
pay."

The alien threw back his head and laughed, the
skin of his neck jiggling and wobbling. He mimed
wiping his eyes, then gave them both a look.

"That the dafest thing I evah heard. If'n you can't
find her, how you s'pposed pay her?"

They looked at one another, making eye contact,
and he sighed, then turned back to the man.

"That's the problem—"

He was about to go on, but the man waved a hand
to cut him off.

"That ain't no problem. If she gone moved her
station, she can't espect you ta pay, can she?"

They looked at one another again, then Bridyant
looked around, conspiratorially, and moved closer to
him.

"We've heard that she isn't a good person to upset. We've heard that she makes people disappear..."

She let it hang, waiting. He gazed at her, blinking, then shrugged.

"Ahh still don' see what I gonna git outta this?"

Stem grabbed his arm, ignoring the sudden glare of hostility, way past caring about it now.

"OK, how about this, how about we promise to help you out, you know, if you ever need anything?"

The alien was still staring at Stem's hand where it gripped his arm, and he let go, stepping back slightly and looking apologetic. The silence stretched out, and Stem wanted to scream, contenting himself instead with sitting and wrapping his hands around the arm rest, clinging on until the knuckles turned white. Eventually, the man shook his head, slowly.

"Ahh could go wit' tha'. You gonna give me yo' dittails afore I give you the co-ords, right?"

They nodded, and he sat back, sighing.

"Aright then. We go in a few, once ah finished ma drink."

His self control slipped.

"No, I'm sorry, we need to go now, right now."

He grabbed his arm and pulled, then Bridyant helped him out and they hauled the protesting alien from his chair, apologising, but being no less insistent. They got him up and walking to the lift, both working hard to rein in their stride.

His ship was huge, a grimy conglomerate of freighter crates welded together and tacked on the back of an engine. The cockpit smelled of use, and, judging by the food packets littering the place, was where he spent the majority of his time. He punched up the co-ordinates, and they checked that they weren't those they already had, then left as quickly as possible, wondering whether they would ever be called on by him to help out, and what it might look like if they were.

An hour later the clamps detached and they floated free, out into space, and headed for Station Nephal.

Chapter 10 - Ally

The chat, it turned out, was more of a rant, Nephal going to great lengths to let her know just how helpless she was, just how long she was going to be there, and how useless all her wonderful power was. The crazy woman clearly didn't realise that being stuck in a giant 'glass cage was far more frightening than being shouted at by someone who looked like they were about to keel over dead. Ally made a great show of yawning, covering her mouth, then closing her eyes and leaning back. This incensed her even more of course, but the ranting soon became a drone, muffled by the thick liquid.

She still wasn't used to being submerged, or trapped, but the need to scream and lash out was fading a little. Replacing it was a burning in her gut, a fire that made her clench her fists and grit her teeth, every muscle straining and tight.

When the thing that put her here walked away, she sank down into a squashed crouch, then slipped out onto the spirit plane. She pressed against the glass and tried to reach through it. She could feel the things within it, the layers it was composed of, and there was one, sliver thin, that was blocking her. She pressed against it and it gave, slightly, then pushed back. It was malleable, not at all like the glass surrounding it, and she focused on it, feeling it. It wasn't solid at all, nor was it manufactured. It felt like a person, like it was alive, and she pushed again. This time it sagged, then shoved back and she was pushed away from the glass. She stared at it, brows creased together, then the quiet voice of Lucid stole into her thoughts.

"Atan tells me you escaped a Homeship?"

She nodded, her chest swelling ever so slightly.

"We killed one of them, too."

She turned to him, unable, and unwilling to keep the savage triumph from her voice. He raised an eyebrow, smiled sardonically and nodded.

"Most impressive, young lady. I will confess to having a deep dislike of that particular species. Call me racist if you will, but I haven't yet met one I would invite over for dinner."

His manner was odd. Where Atan was jovial, and friendly, Lucid seemed almost aloof, set atop a place where he stared down upon everyone. It was nice to know he held the Atrile in particular disdain.

"So, how did you end up here?"

He sniffed, and turned away, staring across the room. She thought for a moment she had offended him, then he turned back to her, and made a 'please, be seated' gesture.

"Atan was, is, an explorer, a discoverer of new things and new places. I, on the other hand, am a thief."

She started, then laughed, shaking her head.

"No, it's true, I assure you. It is a peculiar fact of life that when you tell people you steal things for a living, they become oddly trusting of you, as if you have told them it to suggest you won't steal anything from them."

He shook his head, then returned to his story.

"I work for people, normally very rich ones, who want something badly enough to pay for it. They give me the money, I return with whatever it is they desire. I've taken the teeth from inside the mouth of a living dragon, and stolen the crown from the head of a ruling king. Actually, he was sleeping at the time, and the crown was hanging over the back of the throne, some floors below his bed chamber, but that doesn't have quite the same ring to it.

"My most recent employers wanted a ring, simple, but apparently heavy with sentiment and family history. The lord's wife had run away, hopped a ship with some pirate or other and fled the system. He wasn't too bothered about her return, but she was wearing his grandmother's ring, and that was an entirely different matter.

"It took a few months, but I found her, then tracked her through a few systems. She and her boyfriend were planet-hopping, trying a bit of this and a little of that, never staying long and never getting comfortable. He was, it turned out, something of a professional womaniser, skilled in keeping them sweet and interested, until he got bored.

"I cornered them on a dusty little ball, imaginatively monikered 'six'. It was one of these holiday planets, entirely colonised from outside, and used for the sole purpose of building colossal holiday destinations, complete with every possible pleasure going. He was in the toilet when I approached her, and she knew the game was up when I used her married name.

"Hello Princess Cambria, isn't it just a lovely evening?"

She pushed her chair away and stood up, a rather imaginative look of disdain and ignorance, pre-practiced, and now worn on her not unattractive face. To give her credit, she did try to deny it, though not as convincingly as perhaps she could.

"My dear fellow, I have no clue as to whom you refer. Are you sure you aren't looking for someone else?"

Her voice became louder once I told her she was most certainly the correct person.

"I must request that you desist, and leave me be."

She hissed at me. You might think the term is a figure of speech, that only rats and snakes hiss, but she really did. No words, just a hiss. I began to understand why the lord wasn't too bothered about her return. Her eyes traveled over my shoulder and across the restaurant, and my heart sank as they lit up.

"Jonathon, please, this gentleman is being most rude to me, most rude."

He bristled his way over, paying little mind to the muttering diners he was shoving his way past. His hand rested on his sword. When he came close enough, I felt obliged to introduce myself.

"Jonathon, it is a pleasure to meet you, sincerely. I actually came to speak to the Lady, whom you so carelessly stole from her husband. I must confess, from one thief to another, I thought you did a sterling job, really very professional. Unfortunately, your lady friend has something her husband requires, so if you'd be so kind as to go back to the toilet for another five minutes, then I'll be out of your hair."

"He came at me then, without so much as a hello, which, I suppose, is the most you should expect from a pirate. He was, it turned out, as proficient with that sword as the one in his trousers. Now, I myself have some skill with the blade and blocked his first strike, tumbling back against the table. The lady, predictably, screamed and ran from the room, and I rolled around the table and bought myself a moment to recover. Then, he was on me.

"He leapt to the table top and swung down, a crude blow from which I deftly dodged, before going for his legs. He jumped the cut, but landed badly and fell from the table, onto his shoulder. I stabbed, aiming for his neck, but he rolled and came up, returning fire with a wicked thrust at my stomach. I parried, driving his sword wide and flicked a quick riposte, for which I was rewarded with a grunt and a line of blood across his chest.

"The match went on, the restaurant empty save for the kitchen staff, who had come out to watch, and were absently munching on the leftovers from their departed patrons. I was, I reflected during a lull in the proceedings, getting no closer to retrieving the ring. I was also becoming bored, which was why he landed the next blow. I had scampered back behind a table and was using the opportunity to look out of the restaurant in the vague hope she would still be there. Alas, I stared a little too long, and his next strike caught me unawares.

"It was a lunge, aimed for my heart. I got my blade to it, but only enough to deflect it as far as my shoulder. His blade went in deep and I found myself stuck. I fell backward, off the blade, with a cry of agony, and collapsed on the floor, feigning death.

"He fled, bloodied sword in hand, and I was surrounded by a panicked group of waiters, who tried to pick me up and remove me from the premises. I think they were rather taken aback when I sprung up and ran out of my own accord. Considering that all but the most short-sighted of people would have seen I was struck in the shoulder, I was amazed they would have considered me anything but wounded. The tendency of most people to see what they want to, rather than what is there, still surprises me.

"They headed off-planet, so I jumped in my ship and gave chase. The police were waiting just above the atmosphere, and something resembling a chase began. Fortunately for me, being the second craft, most of them followed the pirate and the lady, leaving me with one, paltry pursuer, whom I lost in short order. In another impressive display of skill, the pirate escaped the police, and I followed him to where else, but here?

"He docked, as did I. I stayed on ship, scouting in the spiritual, and following the two of them around. They spoke to Nephal a couple of times, conversations that seemed entirely innocent. Eventually, I knew my time was running out, and ventured onto the station. I got as far as the central core before I was grabbed, hoodwinked by a bunch of mechanics. They dragged me into her room, where the pirate and the lady waited to gloat as I was dragged through the frame and in here."

He sighed, staring at the doorway that lay behind the frame.

"To this day, I still wonder where the ring is. I can only assume it is still on her finger, on whichever planet he dumped her. As for the pirate..."

He shrugged, then finally turned to look at Ally.

"It is a sad and sorry day that one such as I am tricked and captured, but there it is. So tell me, what is the plan?"

Chapter 11 - Stem

There was a soft thump as they docked, the hatch hissed, and they unbuckled and headed for the hatch. Bridyant put her hand on his arm, just before he pressed the release.

'Remember, Stem, this Nephal, whoever she actually is, has power. Whatever she did to you and Alicia when you were last here, she will attempt again. Be wary.'

'You too.'

Bridyant smiled, and shook her head. 'I do not think I have anything to worry about.'

Stem raised an eyebrow, but his impatience got the better of him. He punched the door release and stepped out into the spoke. The peace of the station was in marked contrast to the cacophony of Gateway. His shoulders dropped and warmth flowed through him, his neck no longer aching as they made their way to the central hub. Nephal's soft voice welcomed them.

"Stem! It's so good to see you here. When you left, we were so worried, and Ally was beside herself. She was sure you had gone to earth without her, and she was so upset. I'm glad you're safe. Who is this with you?"

He found himself speaking out loud, then realised that Bridyant was introducing herself anyway, and took a moment to listen. Nephal's voice was soothing, not at all the patronising tone he had thought he remembered. In fact, everything about the station felt different, as if he'd returned to a slightly different place. She asked them to come and see her straight away, so they walked quickly through the crowds to her room, and presented themselves before the screen.

It flashed gently, the lights calming him even further, then her voice came again.

"Stem, I thought it best to tell you straight away, Ally has left and headed for Earth. She was distraught when you were gone, but felt sure that was where you would have headed. I suggested she wait here, but she was worried you would get there before her and be in danger."

The voice paused, and when it came again, Stem's face turned red.

"She cares for you very much, you are a lucky man."

He coughed, thanked her, and they left. When they stepped out into the corridor, Bridyant touched his arm, making him pause. She looked around, at the travellers making their way around the station, then back at him.

"This place is different than I had thought to find it. It is peaceful, and welcoming."

He caught the implied question all too well and found himself turning red again. He spluttered, then finally shrugged and waved his hands.

"When I was here before, it was different, just... I don't know, maybe I imagined it, maybe it was all in my head, like Ally said. She was right about the spiritual plane..."

He drifted off, thinking about her flying hell bent for leather toward earth, and shook his head. When he turned to Bridyant, his face was set.

"Either way, it doesn't matter now. What matters is getting to the ship and following her. Do we need anything?"

Her response was to shake her head and begin walking, not quite running, to the ship, Stem hot on her heels.

They pulled free of the spoke, and powered up the engines, setting course for Earth. They would pass Gateway and could do a final refuel and LS fill there. For now, he just needed to know they were headed in the right direction.

They were a few minutes into flight, when Bridyant slammed on the reverse engines, stopping the ship almost dead. She turned to Stem, her face furious, teeth bared and he shrank back, putting his hands up before him. She waved a hand in apology, then turned back in her seat, gripping the sticks as she put the throttle up and turned them around.

"Bridyant, what are we doing, what the hell are you doing?"

She spoke through gritted teeth.

"There is something on that station, something that makes us malleable, pliable to whatever it is that Nephal wants us to think. How else do you explain what just happened."

She hissed.

"She tampered with us, Stem, abused our minds. That will not stand."

It was like a curtain had been pulled away, and the pattern he had stared at for the last week was suddenly revealed to be just that, and nothing more. He put his head in his hands, shaking it, then slammed his fists against the arm rests.

"Of course, the entire thing. All our arguments, dammit!"

Bridyant was nodding soberly, putting more and more power through the sticks. They would be back at the station in a few minutes, and he could feel his blood boiling, the familiar taste of bile in the back of his throat as he went over and over it. It was no different to what the Lords had done to them. Seemed like everyone treated humans as people to be pushed around. But she'd done it to Bridyant as well.

And she'd fooled him twice. The first time he could understand, but they had known what to expect going back, and still she'd got them. He was almost too angry to be embarrassed, but his face went red anyway.

"How did you realise? I mean, just now?"

The woman shrugged, glancing back at him with her eyebrows raised.

"I would be inclined to say it was logic. I have been unhappy ever since you told me about the arguments between you and Alicia. They didn't fit with what I know of the two of you. Then the station was different to how you described it, but I didn't find it odd. That was what threw me, once we got far enough away for me to realise. I should have reacted far more strongly, and I didn't, and I couldn't figure out why. The logical reason has to be that there is something, or someone, on the station that is controlling peoples' minds."

The station came into view on the screens and she angled toward it.

"What are we going to say?"

Bridyant tipped her head to one side, then said with a slight chuckle.

"I'm not sure we need to be too concerned about what we say."

She motioned to the cabinet hung at the back of the cockpit.

"Perhaps you should open that and find something for yourself."

He unstrapped and undid the clip, swinging the cabinet door wide. Within, an arsenal awaited him, racks of guns, knives, swords, and a whole bunch of other bladed weapons he had no names for. He looked at her, and saw that she was wearing a fierce grin, as they bore down on the station. He selected a blaster, similar to those the guards on the Homeship had used, and checked that it was fully charged.

They docked, unmolested, and stepped back onto the station again. Nephal made no attempt to contact them, and the station was oddly quiet as they made their way down the corridor, feet echoing loudly on the steel grating. They were only twenty feet from the central hub when the fat alien stepped out and stood in the middle of the corridor, two guns in his four hands, and a sneer plastered across his face.

"You might fink we'd wanna 'ave a chat, but it seems it's a little bit past that now."

He raised a gun, and Stem only had time to blink before the sound of a shot deafened him, ringing around the metal corridor. He realised with some surprise, that it hadn't been the pirate's gun going off, but Bridyant's. The man facing them wore a surprised look, staring down at where his arm had been, now replaced with a smoking stump, his hand and gun some distance behind him. Then he screamed and began to fire with the other one.

His pain made his aim careless at best, and Stem ducked, scrambling backward as bullets thudded into the ceiling. Bridyant was still standing, gun aimed at the man, and her next shot took him through the eye, sending him staggering back, blood streaming from the wound. He dropped to his knees, then fell forward. As if a switch had been flicked, a crowd of beings, all bearing arms, came charging round the corners and began firing.

Within seconds, the corridor was filled with smoke, the muzzle flash like lightning in clouds. The ceiling halfway between Stem and their attackers collapsed, huge sheets of metal clattering to the floor, forming a makeshift barricade. He was stunned to see Bridyant run back toward them and tuck herself behind the metal, then lean out and take a shot.

He shook his head, and ran back to join her, skidding to his knees, breathless. She spared him a glance as he landed.

"Do you know how to fire that thing?"

He nodded, then wobbled a hand before him.

"Uh, yeah, pretty much. Not so sure about the aiming thing though."

She raised an eyebrow, leant out and took a shot, then ducked back in. She was rewarded with a scream of pain from further down the corridor, and she looked at him again.

"There are a number of them, and they are all standing in the same place. They are, I suspect, not used to this sort of thing. Just aim straight down the corridor, and don't get hit."

He nodded, and glanced around the barricade. They were taking turns firing, giving the smoke time to clear to get a decent shot. The metal he was leaning against juddered and slammed back into him, and he stood straight up, bringing his gun over the sheet. He could see where they were standing and took a shot, then dropped. He waited for the screams, but nothing came and he felt oddly deflated.

Bridyant took her shot, then he had another try, this time feeling better about the way they scattered when he emerged. Still no luck, but it gave Bridyant the chance to line up her next shot, and another cry drifted down to them. The noise was ridiculous, the metal frame of the spoke shaking as the gunfire hammered into it. It occurred to him that if they kept going, they might break through the steel plate; he had no idea how strong it was. Sweat streamed from his face, and pooled beneath his arms.

He heard a hiss, then Bridyant grabbed his collar and dragged him backwards. The next moment, all the gunfire and shouting were eclipsed by an explosion that sent the metal barrier flying toward them, driven along by a wall of fire. Bridyant threw him to the ground, diving at the same time, and he gasped as the heat struck him, then the barricade smashed across his back, and he shouted in pain.

She dragged him to his feet, and he got his legs beneath him. He could vaguely hear someone shouting, but his ears were ringing, and he was struggling to balance. He glanced back down the corridor, and saw that more of the ceiling had come down, effectively blocking the way, but smoke had filled the space and was escaping only slowly through the gaps. He ran the other way, until he reached Bridyant's ship, where he paused, gasping for breath. She signalled that he should get down and they both lay on the floor, taking short breaths.

"So, talking, not gonna happen, right?"

She chuckled, shaking her head.

"I fear not. At least we know we're in the right place. They are very keen on us not getting into the central core, which means that is exactly what we need to do."

She put her head back and closed her eyes. He did the same, emerging from his body just after her. She shook her head at him.

"You need to stay here, make sure that we are still safe. I shall only be gone for a moment."

Reluctantly, he slipped back into his body and sat up. The smoke was thinning slightly, but he coughed when he took too deep a breath. The sounds of more gunfire were finding their way into his damaged ears, and he watched the debris shake as they tried to blast their way through.

A few moments later, Bridyant sat up, her expression one of frustration and interest. She stared at the barrier for a moment, then touched his arm.

"I am quite certain that Alicia is still here. There is something, a shield around the central core, where this Nephal lives. I cannot see in, or read anything about anyone living within it. It is, I suspect, a holding cell for people on the spiritual plane, as well as the physical."

"And you're sure she's in there."

Bridyant gave him a patient look, then shook her head slowly.

"I cannot guarantee anything. But I have a hunch, and since that was what led me to finding you, I am inclined, as I have always been, to trust it."

He thought for a moment, wincing and ducking his head as a piece of the barrier shook free and clattered to the floor.

"So, if it's a shield, how come Nephal can go through it?"

"Her screen. I have never seen its like, and would wager that is the device that gives her the ability, not just to interact outside of the core, but also to run the mind-changing magic."

He grinned, nodding.

"So, we get to the screen and trash it, and everything changes?"

"Not everything, but yes, it should definitely make a difference. But how do we get to the screen?"

She waved a hand at the barricade, now beginning to bow and sag beneath the weight of gun fire. Bridyant got closer and peered through a gap, ducking down almost immediately and scuttling back to where he crouched.

"They are not far from the barricade, and there are eight of them..."

Stem suddenly grinned at her.

"How safe do you think the central core is? I mean, will it be sealed?"

She thought for a moment, then nodded.

"I would expect there to be blast doors at the ends of the spokes, that is standard for this sort of station. The core is clearly sealed, also.'

She had already cottoned on to what he was suggesting and gave him the thumbs up with a grin, then scrambled on board her ship. He gave the barrier one more glance, and followed her.

On board, he strapped himself in, then set about arming the forward cannon. She broke the dock and they drifted away, engines ticking over. Using the side thrusters, she gently moved the ship, in tiny increments, until the front swung round to face the join of their spoke with the centre. Stem was pleased to see that most of the other ships had also left, scared away by the gun fire, and now hovered, some distance away, waiting to see what was going to happen next.

He wrapped his hands around the firing column, then squeezed gently, experimenting. The cannon responded more quickly than anything they had on the Vale, and a stream of energy chopped through the end of the spoke. The huge steel tube stayed where it was for a moment, then the movement of the station made it break free and drift. Their attackers came floating out, their faces bloated in the vacuum, guns drifting free from dead hands.

He felt a twinge, a sudden twist in his gut. He hadn't killed many people, and those that he had, deserved it. He knew nothing about these guys, except for what they had done when he'd been there, and they had tried to kill him, but they had been under Nephal's control for years, and there was no telling what effect that would have on someone. He had a flash of lying in the cold, stripped-out space ship and the guilt faded.

He turned to Bridyant.

"Right, let's go dock."

She hauled the ship around, giving it a little more power now, and they docked on the nearest spoke. Just as they were coming in, he saw, nestled in tight to a spoke on the other side of the station, and covered in plastic sheeting, the unmistakable shape of the Vale.

Bridyant handed him an oxygen mask, and he looked at it, then back at her.

"If it isn't pressurised, this isn't going to make much of a difference."

"It will have pressure, I am sure, but we may have hit the air conditioning, or the filters, in which case the air will be most unpleasant, if not entirely poisonous."

He nodded, slipped the mask over his head, picked his gun up and headed out of the ship, Bridyant hot on his heels. The spoke was deserted, and they ran down toward the central hub. They paused where the two joined, looking out into the main area. It was deserted; presumably anyone who had been here was either on their ship or had been sucked out of the spoke before the blast door came down. The read-out on his tank showed that the air was clear and they pulled the masks down, saving the oxygen, then ran toward Nephal's room.

They were nearly there, when a figure dived out from a door in the hub and crashed into him, slamming him to the floor, and landing heavily on top of him. He grunted as the air rushed from his lungs, and his vision went dark for a moment. When it cleared, he had a second to see Bridyant also struggling with someone, rolling on the floor, then the man raised the knife he held and brought it flashing down towards him.

Chapter 12 - Ally

"Huh?"

"You have a plan, do you not, some idea on how we can release ourselves?"

She shook her head, palms up, then stopped herself and looked at the glass, then back at Lucid. He still wore his expression of boredom, but was interested enough to be still watching her. She didn't have a plan, did she? She thought again about how the barrier had felt, when she tried to push through it before, and the beginnings of something blossomed in her mind. She looked at Lucid, then slowly shook her head.

"This glass, that isn't glass? I think I can break through it."

He raised an eyebrow, just a fraction, then placed his hands against it. They sank through the glass and met the living barrier beneath.

"I have tried this myself. It is a construct of the vile woman sat over there. It is remarkably strong, and whilst I have faith in whatever your abilities may be, I would be surprised were you able to break through."

She nodded, putting her own hands on the glass.

"I think it's connected to her. I can feel her in it, and when I push, it pushes back. It's not just a set thing, I think she has to control it. We need to create some kind of distraction, something that puts her under serious stress."

As she said the last word, the entire station rocked, the muffled sounds of cannon fire reaching them in their tanks. Then the room listed to one side and she jerked back into her body, throwing her arms out to brace herself against the sides of the tanks. Moments later, the engines kicked in, and the station righted itself. She slipped back onto the spiritual plane to see Lucid, a smile of real amusement on his face.

"So something like that, you mean?"

She grinned back, and nodded.

"Yeah, that should do it."

She pushed, shoving her whole weight against the barrier, and it sank in, until her hands were outside of the tank. The effort was huge, her mind aching as she struggled against it. It snapped back, throwing her into the tank. She bounced off the other wall and came to hover, staring in frustration at the glass.

"That was closer than anything else I've seen, perhaps if you tried again?"

The explosions had stopped now, and the room was quiet. In the centre, Nephal looked like she'd been stung, her entire face screwed up, her eyes flashing. She was staring at the frame, her hands gripping tightly the rests of her chair. Ally shook her head, then looked at him.

"Give me your power."

"I'm sorry?"

"I don't know, can you, like, give me some of your power, somehow?"

He was looking at her like she had suggested he remain honest for the rest of his life, and she sighed, then turned to Atan. The large alien was watching them, and she pleaded with him.

"Can you do it? I mean, it can't be that difficult, just send me whatever you can."

He shook his head, gesturing at the tank.

"This barrier is effective against all of those sorts of things, I am afraid. But I agree with Lucid, your efforts a moment ago were entirely impressive, just try again."

She shook her head. She couldn't try any harder than that, not and keep her head in one piece. Nephal was speaking, muttering to herself and pacing across the middle of the room. She listened in, her heart beating faster when she heard what she was saying.

"They're attacking my station, how dare they, wretched, pathetic children. How is he still alive?

And why has he come back for her, I thought I made it quite clear."

A smile lit up her face and she turned to Atan. He smiled back.

"So I am going to meet Stem, am I? How marvellous."

She bit her lip, then stared into his eyes.

"Atan. We are going to get out of here, very soon. When we do, Stem and I are going to Earth..."

She fished around, trying to find the right words. She felt young surrounded by these people. They had seen so much, and been to so many places, and she had done nothing except discover a talent that was her's by luck alone. It felt suddenly very important that she find the right way to ask, to pay the proper respect, particularly to the rotund alien who had made her short time here so much more bearable that she thought possible.

"It would be a great privilege, and honour, not to mention help, if you were willing to come with us, to Earth, I mean. I mean, it's fine if you don't, really, I get it. It isn't your fight or anything, just, I think we could really use the help."

She winced, screwing her eyes up and looking at him sideways. She'd started so well. His face broke into the familiar smile, and he laughed.

"It is sweet of you to think that you needed to ask. We are all on board, as it were, with your particular quest. What is more, I think we all have a little more of a sense of what it must feel like to be in your shoes, young lady."

He sighed, settling his hands on his stomach.

"My race believes strongly in the freedom of every being. We detest what the Atrile have done, and were we a more warlike people, we may have contested them, but they grew quickly and once the humans were enslaved they had an almost inexhaustible supply of troops."

He glanced about the room.

"Others here are not so enlightened, and view your race as border people, no more deserving of their freedom than livestock. I am happy to say that your story has changed minds, and people. That, and the time spent in here. Once people have had a genuine taste of confinement, of being subjugated and having no say in the matter, their opinions are wont to change. What Nephal has done here is a microcosm of what the Atrile have done with the human race. Beings who have spent their lives in freedom have a new understanding."

She interrupted, "Sorry, what do you mean, my story? I haven't spoken to any of the others."

He shook his head.

"Of course not, communication between us has been only possible to those on either side, but I have taken great pleasure in telling Fadern Dill, the gentleman to my right, who in turn passed it to his neighbour, and so on. Knowing how these things work, those opposite us may have an entirely different story, but we shall, I hope, soon see."

"Oh."

"Needless to say, the message coming back is that when you leave here, we shall be coming with you, and we shall be joining you in making a change to the status quo."

She nodded, mutely. It kept getting bigger, and now she was involved in some change in the universe, in a rebellion far larger than anything she had previously dreamed of! She was shaking, wanting to go back to just her and Stem, to a time when it was about them being free, just that. It could still happen. She could get out of here and find him and they could fly away and never see anyone else again. They could go to 'six', and have a holiday.

The dream didn't last. She looked at Atan and saw the fire in his eyes and felt it start in her stomach and spread out until her entire body was aflame, and her fists were clenched and her mind was reeling. She had butterflies racing around inside her, but they were burnt up by the fire until all she felt was the warmth.

She jerked back as Nephal began to scream, a high-pitched keening that cut through her spirit and made her gasp. She retreated into her body in the hope it would ease it, but it got no better and she came back out, pressing against the barrier. The crazy woman was staring at the door to her chamber, the veins in her head popping out, her hands by her sides, clawing at the air.

The sound of a shot, then another, close by, echoed through the chamber, and Nephal's screams grew louder. Ally watched her, transfixed by the rage and fear fighting for domination on her face. Then another shot came, and the scream cut off, their captor collapsing abruptly to the floor. She was moaning, a low wailing escaping her as she rocked.

When she came to her feet, her eyes were flashing, her hands now clenched in fists. She strode to the door and flung it open, leaving the room for the first time since Ally had entered. Next to her, Atan's voice was higher than usual, insistent and excited.

"Now, Ally, now."

She looked at him, confused for a moment, then it sank in and she leaned against the barrier, and pushed.

Chapter 13 - Stem

He twisted, and the knife sliced through his shirt and skimmed his arm, raising a shout as it slammed into the metal floor. The knife was lodged in a gap in the grating and the man wrestled with it, trying to pull it free. Stem punched him in the chest, then, seeing it have no effect, lifted the oxygen canister from beside him and brought it crashing across the side of his head. His attacker rolled off him and onto the floor, and Stem rolled with him, coming up onto his knees and bringing the canister crashing down on his face.

The alien had blue tufts of fur sprouting randomly from his face, like he'd shaved in the dark, all over, but looked otherwise human. He had recovered enough to raise a hand, and it was catching the majority of the blows. With his next strike, he felt the hand break and the man screamed, then swung with his other hand, catching Stem in the face and sending him sprawling. The alien rolled and pushed himself to his feet, shattered hand cradled close to his stomach, other hand reaching for the knife.

As he bent to grab it, Stem stepped in and swung his foot, kicking him hard in the stomach and he went to his hands and knees, grunting. Stem swung at him again, but he pushed away, falling onto his side and Stem overbalanced, falling forward. The man grabbed his leg and hauled and Stem hit the floor, landing awkwardly on his knees, then toppling onto his face. He heard the man scramble up, his boots pounding against the floor that vibrated against his face, and Stem pushed himself up, turning just in time to avoid the knife again, as it swung round in a wide arc.

He scampered backward, bringing up the canister as defence, blocking the next swing and sending the man stumbling past him. He spun, quickly and took the initiative, swinging the canister at the broken hand the man put out to steady himself. It connected with a crack, and he screamed, knife dropping from his hand as he wrapped it around the injured limb. Stem swung again, putting everything he had behind it and smashed the alien around the head. This time, he dropped to the ground and lay still.

Stem dropped the canister, putting his hands on his knees and breathing hard. He looked around and saw Bridyant sliding a knife across her attacker's throat. She walked past him and, before he could say anything, did the same to the man he had just knocked out. He put a hand to his mouth, then bit his tongue. He wanted to shout at her, ask why the hell she'd done it, but he lived in a different world, a world he should have realised no longer existed.

Instead he nodded at her, and saw the almost imperceptible nod she gave in return, the mark of one warrior to another. He almost laughed, then put his hand to the tear in his shirt, realising that he was bleeding, the warm flow trickling down his side. She came over and pulled the shirt out the way, then smiled and shook her head.

"You've been scratched, I wouldn't worry too much."

She glanced down at the bodies, then scanned the corridor.

"Let us hope that was the last of them."

It seemed to be, as they arrived at the door to Nephal's room unmolested. They pushed it aside. Stem was shoved back as the blast went over his head, the heat of it scorching his face. He lay half out of the door, and saw Bridyant dive into the room, then he found himself staring at the barrel of a gun.

He could see the man's knuckles tensing as he squeezed the trigger, and the world seemed to slow down. He took a breath, holding it as his eyes zoomed in on the darkness of the barrel, waiting for the roar. When it went off, he threw his hands up, but the impact never came.

Bridyant had grabbed their attacker by the wrists and they were both straining to take control of the gun. Bridyant was shorter than the man, but clearly just as strong. Stem scrambled to his feet, and entered the room, letting the door close. He saw Bridyant's feet come off the floor and she was shoved backwards, toppling over.

He shouted, then watched in awe as she ran up her attacker, her feet walking up his legs then up to his chest, by which time she had pulled his hands over and above her, the gun now pointing at the wall. She put one foot through his chin and used the other to kick away from his chest. The gun was wrenched from his grasp as he fell back, and she kept moving, flipping entirely to land on her feet, gun in hand.

The roar was loud again as Nephal's bodyguard received two shots, both to the face, and collapsed to the floor. He was shaking his head as he leaned against the wall.

"Where did you learn to do that?"

She shrugged, then looked vaguely sheepish.

"I haven't ever done that before."

He shook his head again, then rocked back as a scream cut through his mind. They pushed through the second door and into Nephal's chamber, where the screen was flashing wildly. She was shouting, high-pitched and wild, obscenities and wordless cries. He had his hands over his ears, but the noise was loud inside his head, inescapable. Bridyant, apparently more sensitive than him, was doubled over, face tense and teeth gritted.

He reached out and took the gun, which she relinquished willingly, motioning with her head to the screen. He nodded, raised it and fired. It shattered, and fell into thick shards of glass that clattered and clashed to the ground, the light that had moved now trapped in the glass. A cloud of dust rose up, and as it settled he could see tiny, multi-coloured shards littering the floor.

He went to step through the frame, when a figure emerged, still ranting and screaming, but now in a voice that was unmistakably human. He stared at her, searching amongst the long gray hair, and wrinkled skin for something that marked her as an alien, but there was nothing. She was human.

He wanted to lash out at her, shout and tell her that he and Ally had been searching for someone like her, someone who could help instead of hinder, someone proud of their humanity instead of hiding it behind a screen. He was about to speak when the screaming began again inside his head, and fingers seemed to wrap around his spirit, pulling him from his body.

He knew no way to resist and was dragged out, hovering before her. He glanced to the right and saw Bridyant, beads of sweat now dripping down her leathery face. Nephal seemed to have forgotten him for a moment, in her struggle with his friend, and he rushed in spirit form past her and into her chamber.

He gasped as he saw the glass tanks, and spied Ally across the room. Her eyes were closed as he flew across, and as he got there, she came into being right before him. He flew into her arms and they embraced, minds touching and feelings swimming between them. She pushed him. A huge grin split her face.

"You're here, I mean, on the spiritual plane."

He grinned back, and nodded."

"Look, Ally, I'm so sorry."

She waved it away, eyes leaving his to travel around the chamber.

"No time, and not necessary, really. Sorry, I've got to help the others."

She flew from him, slipping into the nearest tank, then emerging moments later with an alien, in spirit form, held in her arms. The creature was grotesquely fat, and tiny, no more than four feet tall, and nearly circular in shape. He wore a huge smile and stretched, then hugged her. She shrugged it off and dived into the next tank. Stem suddenly felt himself dragged out of the room, and had just enough time to scream her name as he went.

Outside, Nephal's body was leaning against the wall. His and Bridyant's were lying on the floor where they had been standing. The station owner stood, her avatar considerably more attractive and frightening than her physical self, with a hand wrapped around Bridyant's throat. The alien was fuming, her hands clawing the woman, but she was being brushed off, and looked weak before the rage of their attacker.

As he was pulled to stand before her, her eyes flashed and she smiled at him.

"So I get the pair of you, how splendid. Your girl-friend would have been enough, but there's no harm in having both."

He was preparing a come-back, when her face fell, and it was his turn to smile. He saw Ally emerge from the frame, then Bridyant fell from Nephal's hand as she spun.

"How did you—"

She was cut off as Ally put her hands on her shoulders, then the two of them hurtled out of the station, straight up and through the ceiling. Stem yearned to chase them, but instead dropped back into his body and ran through the frame. The inner core was hot, steam misting the fronts of some of the tanks. Bridyant came in behind him and stood, open mouthed, before grabbing his arm.

"This is life support. We must be careful not to switch anything off before we are sure we can get them out. Which one is Alicia?"

He ran across the cable-strewn floor to the tank furthest from them, and swept his hand across the glass, revealing Ally hanging in the strange liquid.

"They had to be put in there, so how do they do it?"

They examined the tank, finding a set of clips down one side, and he flicked them open. Bridyant leapt out of the way as the glass front swung open and the liquid poured out. She waded back into the water and grabbed Ally as she tumbled out of the cabinet. She pulled her up onto the platform that ran around the edge of the room, and laid her gently on her side, the liquid streaming from her mouth.

They moved to the next tank, wiping away the condensation, then lowering their gaze until they found the round alien that Ally had released onto the spiritual plane. Bridyant looked at Stem, eyes wide, and he raised his eyebrows at her.

"This is an elder, from a race I didn't even know still existed. I wonder how long he's been here?"

"So, do we want to release him?"

She laughed, and nodded firmly.

"His people, along with the other elder races, ruled the universe many thousands of years ago, in a time when there were no border races, no subjugation of the weaker planets.' She paused. "I never thought to meet one. This is most exciting."

He laughed at her uncharacteristic excitement, then turned back to the tank. They unclipped it, and caught him as he fell. He was still for a moment, then coughed, sitting up and wiping the thick liquid from his eyes.

He looked at them both, then smiled at Stem.

"And you must be Stem. Splendid! What a pleasure to meet you, thoroughly delightful, I must say."

He leaned forward on the platform, extending his hand and Stem shook it, liking him already. The rotund alien turned to Bridyant, another smiled broadening his already wide face.

"An Eltarch, splendid! It has been many a long while since I met one of your race. Still searching for knowledge, I hope."

Bridyant smiled in return, and bowed slightly.

"Always, Elder, always. It is an honour—"

"Nonsense. All you know about me is that I was stupid enough to get myself caught by that fiend who calls herself Nephal. In truth, you should probably scorn me, and leave me here to fend for myself."

He glanced across at Ally's prone body.

"Is she alright?"

Stem nodded.

"I think she's sorting out the fiend."

Another grin broke out, and Stem found himself grinning along.

"Splendid! So, shall we release the others?"

They made their way around the chamber, opening the cases and placing their occupants around the shelf. One by one they came to, and soon the chamber was full, fifteen captives all wiping themselves clean of the foul liquid in which they had been encased.

They were waiting, he realised, and he turned back to Ally. She was cold and he wrapped his arms around her, whilst Bridyant searched the chamber. She found a small door, tucked away behind the central chair, and within it was a small chamber, housing amongst other things, some clothes. She came out with blankets and they wrapped Ally up, Stem rubbing her hands as she lay with her head in his lap.

He turned to Bridyant. 'We should help her, could you find her, and help?'

The grey alien nodded, and sat, before her body relaxed as she slipped free. Stem looked around the room at the others, strange beings coming slowly back to life. How long had they been here? He looked back down at Ally, her pale face looking so tired, so lost. He waited, squeezing her tight against him, as though he could somehow help her fight just by loving her. Silence fell in the chamber, as one by one, the others stilled, all eyes on the prone body he held in his arms.

Chapter 14 - Ally

It was seeing him that did it, seeing him and feeling the rush that ran through her, the butterflies
that had swamped her when they bumped into one
another for the first time. They were still there,
only now they flew in harmony with her, the tight-
ness in her gut replaced with a savage need, a
yearning to hold him. And the barrier parted.

She rushed through and into his arms, their
emotions bleeding into one another so she forgot
where she ended and he began. She held him as
hard as she could, then she felt something that
broke through her reverie. She could hear Nephal,
feel the power rushing from her.

She freed Atan, and was moving to Lucid's tank
when she heard Stem's strangled cry. She flew
across the room and through the door, seeing
Nephal's back, and beyond her, Bridyant! Nephal
spun,

"How did you—"

Not giving her time to finish her sentence, or do
anything worse, Ally grabbed her under the arms

and dragged her up and out of the station. As they emerged into space she threw her, sending her flying across the blackness, twisting and shrieking. She charged after her and grabbed a foot, stopping her dead, then pulled her closer so they could see eye to eye.

"I don't know you. I thought I knew you, but there is nothing human inside you."

Nephal lashed out, catching her across the face with one bony hand. The station master shouted at her, a wordless cry, then spoke softly.

"How can you, of all people, question me? You came here from the Homeship, just as I did."

Nephal looked down at her feet, then raised her head again.

"We spent our lives as slaves, you and I. How can that happen to us and no one care? How can this universe, filled with such wisdom and love, turn its back on a race being enslaved? THEY ABANDONED US!"

She was heaving, her whole body racked by the emotions that were finally spilling out.

"They have no rights, not anymore. They deserve their freedom no more than the Atrile, no more than anyone willing to turn away from the pain we have suffered."

Ally broke in.

"But why me? I've already been a slave, and I know better than anyone what it means to be trapped, held hostage. Why me?"

Nephal's face became sly, and she giggled, her entire body changing abruptly, becoming languorous and lazy.

"You, I must confess, were just for the fun."

She held her hands up as if she held Ally's face between them.

"You have such power, so intense, so fresh. I just couldn't resist."

She shrugged and giggled again. Ally felt the sympathy that had been growing in her vanish, replaced by the vague need to vomit, then, far stronger, the urge to hit her. She was opening her mouth to speak, when Nephal pulled a dagger from behind her back, tucked in her robes, and flew at Ally.

She put her arm in the way and their wrists smacked together. The pain was surprising, and for a moment they grappled, the knife close to her face. Then she caught herself, remembering where they were, and she stared at the knife until it became soft, and ran down Nephal's arm, a liquid mess of steel and wood. The woman screamed, grabbing at her hand, and Ally's nostrils wrinkled at the smell of burning flesh. She hadn't meant to make it hot, but actually, how else was it going to melt?

She was reminded that things on the spiritual plane still seemed to obey certain rules of the physi-

cal, before Nephal was throwing herself at her, and
she raised her giant, invisible hand, grabbing her
and holding her at a distance. She bit the inside of
her mouth, doing anything she could to help maintain her calm, and to keep the hand from crushing
closed.

"Nephal, you need to go away from here, far away
to a place you can forget where you came from. You
need to forget the Atrile, and find peace within
yourself, because right now, you are as much a slave
to them as you were when you lived on the
Homeship."

She didn't know where the words came from,
but they felt true, and she recognised them as
things she needed to say to herself as well. She had
wondered earlier whether earth was actually her
home, whether going there was going to be everything she hoped. And now, as she told Nephal the
truth, she understood that going to earth could only
be about destroying the Atrile, because until she
had, she was still a slave, and nowhere would be
home, not really.

Nephal was spitting, incoherent rage and guttural
words that meant nothing. Ally tried again.

"I'm going to put you back in your body and give
you a ship, and you need to leave, OK?"

The words became suddenly clear.

"I'm going to kill you, you and everyone else in that room, you don't deserve to live, I'll kill you, I'll kill you."

She broke free of the hand and flew across the gap between them, hands held out like claws. Ally didn't even think. Before she knew it, Bridyant's sword was clenched in her fist and sliding into Nephal's body, under her ribs and up into her heart. Her shouting stopped abruptly, replaced with a gasp. Her eyes were open, inches from Ally's and tears appeared in them, though didn't escape.

"You are all slaves, every one of you. I was free."

Her head lolled to one side, and Ally pushed the body away, shaking and flapping with her hands. She went cold, rubbing the back of her neck and her face, as if to scrape away the prickling and goose-bumps. She stared at the body, floating, hunched over. Nephal's long hair was hanging down, obscuring the sword that thrust out from her chest, then her body faded, and Ally was alone.

Moments later she jerked in his lap as she dropped back into her body, then coughed, spitting out liquid that splattered on the floor, and sat up. She blinked, then looked into his eyes, and burst into tears. He wrapped his arms around her and held her and after a few moments, she hugged him back, her tears fading away.

As she huddled in his embrace, tears drying on her cheeks, she remembered Nephal's last words. She looked up at Stem, blinking.

'She was mad, Stem, and she came from a Homeship.'

His eyes widened as he glanced across the room to the broken screen. 'Is she dead?'

Ally nodded. 'I tried, I tried to get her to go away, but she...' She trailed off. 'She thought everyone was against her, she must have been so lonely.'

She gripped him tight, burying her face in his chest.

Outro

They left the station on four ships, the Vale, Bridyant's, and two other cruisers that were still moored there. Some of those who had fled when the shooting started were already returning, docking and wandering through the empty station. They left Nephal's body where it had dropped, in the frame where her screen had shattered.

They had two others on the Vale, Atan and Lucid, and the rest were spread out on the other three. They drifted free of the station, gunned the engines and set course for Gateway.

She was trying to get used to the idea that they had help, others who wanted the same as them, and were willing to fight for it. That this had become bigger than her, so much more than what she and Stem had talked about back in the engine room, hadn't escaped her notice. She just hoped she could deliver what she had promised, that the spell the Master had given them would work.

They were less than a day from the giant station, and she barely had time to catch up with Stem before it appeared, a distant speck on the screens. As they cruised closer, she noticed a number of larger ships were crowded around the station, then she felt something, something that made her skin crawl and her head hurt.

The ships were horribly familiar, and they weren't docked, they were positioned in a cordon around Gateway. Six Homeships, the one nearest them facing out into space, and straight at them. Then the voice, a sound she had hoped never to hear again, crawled inside her brain.

"Hello, Alicia. I thought we told you to run. It seems you didn't run quite far enough."

A Game of War
Book Six

Gateway To
Earth

Intro

"Oh, hell, oh no, no."

She slammed on the thrusters and the Vale lurched, then jumped forward. From the cabin she heard Lucid grunt as he was thrown onto the floor. Atan grabbed her chair just in time, swinging round on one foot as they accelerated. She leaned on the sticks and took them down, and away from the Homeships.

"They're launching, we've got pursuers."

Stem was staring wide-eyed at the screens, one hand resting lightly on the firing stick. She saw from the corner of her eye his other hand tracing the paths of the emerging fighters. On another screen, Ally watched as Bridyant and the others also switched course, sticking with her. Stem gave feedback, though Ally barely heard it, letting herself slip into the spiritual, her hands moving unconsciously on the sticks.

"OK, there's about ten of them, all small, all heading straight for us."

Bridyant's voice came through the communications link.

"Do we fight?"

"I don't know, let me check with Ally. We can take them, four against ten."

"I agree. Ally?"

She dragged herself back to her body, blinking, then staring again at the screens. Every part of her was screaming that they should run, just get out, but they had precious little air, and she didn't want to run, not anymore.

Chapter 15

"They'll be humans, gamers just like we were, disabling shots only. Did everyone get that?"

Murmurs of assent came through from the others, and she slipped out again. Stem joined her, their minds coming together, and she managed a quiet warning to Atan.

"You'll wanna find somewhere to sit."

The next second, the Vale stopped dead, then spun around, leaving the others to race past. She dragged the nose up and they were hurtling toward their pursuers on the angle, coming up underneath. She twitched the nose and he fired the front cannon, the first shot tearing an engine clean out the back of their nearest attacker. She rolled back again, coming cockpit to cockpit, and the rockets streamed out, crashing through the wings of another ship, sending it spinning, helpless.

She was aware of the others now joining the fray. Bridyant was predictably smooth and efficient as her guns took the nose of one of the enemy, leaving it direction-less, charging out into space. The other ship, crewed by people she still barely knew, but fighting beside her nonetheless, were equally impressive, and within minutes, the numbers were level.

A thought found its way through the battle haze, so audacious she felt Stem shiver as he caught it. She felt Atan also, hovering on the spiritual plane, observing, and she spoke to him.

"Contact Bridyant, tell her we're going for a Homeship."

She felt his surprise, then his smile and turned her attention back to the fight. The remaining slaves had split up, one trailing after them, but staying far enough back to avoid any sudden manoeuvres she might try. She reached out, feeling the mind of the pilot, only to realise he almost had a lock on them. Seconds later, he fired and she yanked the Vale into evasive action, rolling left and down, the cannon fire passing wide of them.

As she spun and danced, she was impressed that he stayed back, not allowing himself to be pulled into the pattern. She spread her awareness and found Bridyant, also being pursued, though more clumsily, by a one-man-er.

"Bridyant, how about we help each other out?"

"Come past my right side and across my nose, nice and close."

Ally angled the Vale down, then fell into step with Bridyant, the two ships only metres apart.

Once her pursuer had come around behind, she accelerated and pulled in front of her friend. She watched in the screen as her attacker failed to take the bait, keeping well clear of Bridyant and instead firing another shot that fell just low of their belly. She hissed, struggling to find her focus, but as she pulled back toward Bridyant, the one-man-er dropped into their sights. Stem took the back of the ship off with a cannon shot.

"Thank you both, now perhaps we can deal with your opponent."

Bridyant had maintained her course, but now swung abruptly, coming around sharply to aim straight for the enemy ship. The pilot seemed surprised by the manoeuvre and bolted, cutting across Ally's line. Stem used a rocket to trash the engines and as quickly as it had started, the battle was over. Ten slave ships hung motionless in space, smoke making globes around tattered engines.

Ally turned her attention to the Homeship that had sent the attackers, and leaned on the sticks. The other Homeships would attack soon, the humans on board even now clambering into their cockpits. They had minutes at best. Bridyant fell in beside her, and the massive bulk grew larger and larger until it filled the screens. Bridyant spoke through the comms.

"I have every faith in you, Alicia, but this feels a little rash. Do you have any kind of plan?"

"Aim for the top deck, and don't get shot."

The alien barked a laugh, and gunned her engines, forcing Ally to pick up the pace. Her mind had been distracted during the fight, too interested in what the others were doing, but now her thoughts fell away as Stem's mind joined once more with hers. It was all so simple, just the Homeship, and the hatred and frustration.

The hatches on the side opened, the snub-like barrels emerging, and she realised how utterly ludicrous this was. The first flashes of light came from the guns, and bolts of energy came flying toward them.

They began to dance, spinning and looping around the constant rain of fire. They were close, one blast catching the very tip of the Vale's top fin and wrenching the sticks from her hands. Almost immediately she had them again and brought the ship under control, flicking it vertical to avoid another rocket. She was completely outside her body, her spiritual self merged with Stem's, and controlling as if with a remote, all conscious thought gone.

Bridyant had gone straight up, above the majority of the gun fire, and she chased her, pushing the Vale to go faster and faster. The guns tracked them, but in the clearer space above the Homeship they had time to breathe, and prepare. Their ships were dots against the vast bulk, barely noticeable, but they had been noticed. The voice that had been oddly silent suddenly came howling back into her mind.

"Nothing you can do will change the fate of you or your race. Your actions are futile, this is the time to surrender, to give yourself up. Alicia, I can spare you from the worst of your pain, stop this now."

She grinned, hearing the sound of doubt in a voice ill-used to expressing it. Tipping the Vale down slightly, she gave Stem the green light, and the remainder of their rockets sped toward the top deck, followed swiftly by Bridyant's.

They waited as the ship shot past beneath them, breath held, then the first one struck and a scream tore through their minds. She whooped, a fierce surge of joy from Stem almost knocking her out, and spun the Vale around and headed back down the Homeship. Where the rockets had struck, the top of the ship was torn open, debris flushing out into space.

She searched, questing silently into the wreckage, but found no trace of the creature. She thumped her hand against the stick, a wonderful warmth spreading through her. She pulled the Vale away from the Homeship, and out into space, the other three coming to join her. As she became aware again, she realised that the other Homeships, four in total, had broken free of Gateway and were gathering. The warmth left her and she felt Stem's belief drain away.

"We can't fight that many, Ally, we got lucky but we can't fight them."

She nodded, kicking the steering column, and wincing when Bridyant's voice, still full of confidence, came through.

"What is the plan now?"

She stared at Stem, who shrugged.

"I don't know. I don't know, I'm sorry."

She imagined the Homeship's arsenal - hundreds of cannon and rockets - all turning and taking aim. This time there was no sneak attack. She closed her eyes, and swallowed hard.

Chapter 16

The comms crackled into life, an unfamiliar voice coming through.

"Attention all combatants. This is Gateway. Conflict this close to our station is unacceptable. Should it continue, we will have no choice but to intervene. Should any of you require a place of safety, Gateway is open to any needing it. Violence on board the station will not be tolerated."

The comms clicked, silence falling over the ships. She stared at the screens, one nail held firmly between her teeth, eyes fixed on the Homeships. When the first one moved, she bit straight through the nail, jerking her head as she grabbed for the sticks. It wasn't until she realised it was breaking off, turning slowly away, that she let out the breath she had been holding. Stem flicked on the comms.

"Gateway, this is the Vale hailing. We request permission to dock."

The voice sounded slightly smug, and definitely pleased to hear from them.

"Vale, permission granted, uploading the location to your computer now. Nice to have you with us."

There was a pause, then the voice came back.

"I would enjoy a meeting with you, once you have had a chance to rest."

"Thank you, it would be a pleasure."

He flicked the comms off, looking over at Ally with a worried look.

"I guess?"

She laughed, giggling as the tension drained from her. Lucid carried his tall frame out of the cabin, thin face green and shoulders tense. He looked at her for a moment, then shook his head, and slumped against the wall. Atan, struggling to get his huge bulk up from his snug in between the door and the cabin, chuckled and slapped him on the leg.

"Nothing like a good fight to get your appetite going, eh?"

Lucid glared at him, then rubbed his eyes with his hands. She looked at Atan, clearly looking confused.

"I fear our dour friend feels a little sick, on account of you doing things most pilots would be terrified just thinking about."

He waggled a finger from one to the other.

"The two of you are flying it together, am I correct?"

She nodded, grinning at Stem. Atan clapped his chunky hands together, beaming.

"Splendid, what a fabulous thing to do. I confess it is entirely new to me, but it obviously works."

They couldn't help grinning, smiles that widened at another groan from Lucid. Atan gestured at the screens.

"Should we not go and dock, perhaps?"

She nodded, spinning back to the sticks, and took them in.

The Station was massive, and despite Stem's attempts to describe it, she was still open-mouthed at the sheer scale of the place. It was officially night time now, and the main lights were dimmed. A million tiny bulbs, all different colours and sizes, lit the hall, scattered along the edges and tops of platforms, covering booths and signs and even some of the hawkers' hats. It was magical, like everyone was celebrating a hundred different things at the same time.

They walked slowly through the crowds. Atan kept up a running commentary, having spent many visits here, whilst Lucid would occasionally interject and identify travellers around the place and the myriad ways he had stolen all manner of things from them. The effect was compelling, a world of the new made real through such subjective experiences.

They had reached the escalator and were readying themselves to head up, when a voice slithered into her brain, and she spun, one hand gripping

Stem's arm. Across the hall, and with a large space all around them, two of the Atrile were walking slowly through the station.

"Ally, we are all together here, all bound to peace. What a wonderful opportunity for us to get to know one another better. Please, won't you join us for a drink?"

She stopped short of spitting on the floor, instead turning and stepping onto the escalator. Stem was already on, his face pale and hands shaking where they gripped the rail. She put a hand on his arm, making eye contact, before she turned, staring back. They had stopped, their glittering eyes boring into her. She turned away, her good humour at the wonderful surroundings gone entirely.

She couldn't believe those things were accepted here, roaming around free. Then she thought about the station master asking to meet with them, and she wondered whether what had seemed kind initially might in fact be something else entirely. The idea chilled her, and she moved up a step and pressed against Stem, wrapping her arms around his shaking body.

Bridyant led them up a series of escalators, stairs and lifts until they emerged near the top of the hall, on a platform that ran along one entire side. It was a couple of metres wide and empty, but provided access to doors scattered along the wall at odd intervals. They walked until they came to a door bearing a pale green line drawing of a tree set against grey the exact colour of Bridyant's skin.

She pushed it open and they stepped into a large room lined with sofas and chairs. Bridyant waved them in, and closed the door behind them.

"As part of our sponsorship, we have rooms. Nothing especially smart, but a place to stay, away from the noise."

She waved at some doors on one wall.

"There are beds, if anyone wishes to sleep."

The others spread out, finding places to relax. Three of them, aliens whose names she had only vaguely caught in the rush to leave Nephal, nodded to her, then went straight back out. Bridyant turned to the two of them and spoke more softly.

"I am not sure we'll see them again. They are less invested in this cause and more inclined to get back to their people."

Ally turned back to the door, that familiar sting of disappointment rearing its head. Bridyant must have seen something on her face.

"Try not to be too harsh, Alicia. They have their own stories, their own worlds."

Bridyant was right, and she nodded to show she understood. She glanced around at those who were left. Atan and Lucid were engaged in conversation, but the others, Fadarn and a compact, muscled alien called Driver were sprawled out, eyes closed.

"How about the others?"

Bridyant shrugged, but looked confident.

"They have come this far, I would be surprised if you lost them. Also, they have taken part, be it unwillingly, in a direct assault on the Atrile. I am not sure any would be keen to leave here without protection. It will be safer with us, than without."

Ally looked at the grey-skinned alien.

"Us?"

She smiled, holding out her clenched fist for Ally to tap.

"I am with you now, for the whole journey. I said to you on the Nexus that I believed we were meant to meet, and I was right. Finding Stem the way I did was proof of that."

She nodded at him.

"By rights, you should be floating dead in space, but something sent me in the right direction. I have been taught that these signs, these coincidences, are the things we must take notice of, for they are what guides us down the right paths."

Ally was nodding, then stopped and shook her head.

"But I was so sure that Nephal was the right path, that she was someone who was going to help us."

Bridyant nodded. "It is easy to become confused between coincidence and truth. When you want something badly enough, you can manufacture all the circumstances to fit it."

She put a hand on Ally's shoulder, and squeezed, then Stem spoke.

"Also, we're pretty certain there was something else going on on the station. Something she was doing on the spiritual plane, or maybe even magic. Somehow she made us believe her, and act different."

Ally shrugged, twisting up her face.

"It's easy to say that, but couldn't we be thinking that, just to excuse how we treated each other? I mean, isn't that what you meant, Bridyant? You can find excuses for anything if you look hard enough."

The alien laughed and squeezed her shoulder again. "It is, but in this case, Stem is right. I'm sure there was something else at work, a charm in all likelihood. Be aware of fooling yourself, but try to have faith as well."

Ally nodded, and wandered off to find a bed. She pushed into the nearest room, and collapsed onto the mattress, her eyes closing before she took her boots off.

She didn't know long she'd been asleep, but when the door swung open and Stem bustled in, shaking her leg to wake her, she felt like someone had filled her head with glue, and her mouth with iron filings. She groaned and sat up, giving him a look she hoped carried the right amount of warning. He grinned broadly at her, either oblivious, or choosing to be, and then gave her a kiss.

"Hey sleepy, we've just got a call from the guy who runs this place. He's asked us to go and see him."

"Right now?"

He nodded. "Uhuh. Bridyant thinks it's a pretty big deal. Not many people get to say hi to the guy who owns Gateway."

"Oh joy."

She stood, scrubbed her face with her hands, and stepped back out into the room. Bridyant sat cross-legged at the far end, her eyes closed. Stem put a finger to his lips and they crept from the room, out into the main hall.

Morning had happened whilst she slept and the lights were up full, the noise almost deafening. The directions were simple, and they climbed back into the lift, and hit the button for the top floor. Minutes later, the doors slid open. When they closed behind them, the noise fell away, and they were left in a huge open space, the roof of which was glass. Above them, the spokes and gantries of Gateway stretched up and out, a maze of metal set against the vastness of space.

She stood for a moment, staring up. The stirring in her stomach, she recognised now as excitement, as the rush of potential. Atan's words came back to her, the promise of worlds and stories, so many places she had never been. She turned to Stem, and reached out her hand, searching for his feelings. All she found was Earth, filling his mind, somewhere out there, waiting for his return.

She let his hand fall, the tingling fading as quickly as it had started. He turned and grinned at her and she returned it, hoping he didn't see how much effort it took. She was saved from further introspection by the figure marching toward them.

"Welcome, welcome to Gateway. Like the view, do you?"

He was remarkably human in almost every way, just the protruding lump in the back of his head giving him away. She couldn't stop herself from staring at it, her first thought being that his neck must be in agony. He caught her staring and rubbed it absently with one hand.

"Our movement, basic motor skills and such, are housed in a different place from most. No idea why."

He gestured up to the roof.

"We used to have the hall open up to here, but safety issues and the like forced our hand. It's peaceful here, most of the time, but with this many people, and so many different races crammed in together, you're bound to get problems now and then. Speaking of which..."

He gestured for them to follow, then strode across the hall, both of them hurrying to keep up. He led them into an office, through a door she noticed was thick, and sealed behind them. Sitting himself behind an enormous desk, he waved them into chairs, and bashed a few buttons in the desk. The centre of it split apart, and a pole rose from the middle. Once it had extended fully, it split, falling into two halves, from which more, ultra-thin poles extended. Light flickered between the different poles, then the entire thing lit up and Ally found herself staring at a bank of screens, sixteen in total, all showing views of the hall and platforms.

The captain had disappeared from view, but now came around the side of the screen bank.

"We monitor as much as we can, stepping in before things happen, where possible."

He reached over and pressed another button and every screen flipped, showing her another set of views, those from his side of the desk. He gestured toward one in particular, and she put her arms around herself as she recognised the hulking insect-like beings.

"Of course, sometimes trouble starts outside the station, and there is little we can do then."

He dragged his chair around the desk and sat where he could see them.

"You successfully attacked a Homeship in a two-man fighter, and had another pilot crazy enough to join you. You are humans, free humans with, I can only assume, some basic grasp of the spiritual plane, and you travel with, amongst others, a martial El-tarch and an Elder, from a race most believe to be extinct. It is rare that I'm surprised, but you have done exactly that, on a phenomenal scale. Thank you."

He grinned at them, and they looked at one another, then grinned back. She was waiting for the other shoe to drop, for the first signs that this was going to go the way every other meeting they'd had since escaping the Homeship went. She thought about what Bridyant had said and tried to home in on her instinct. What did this feel like, was he really a good guy? But there was nothing, no signs, just the repeating mantra that trusting anyone was a recipe for disaster. Bridyant made it sound so easy, so natural. Hah, not yet, not for her.

She waited. He was watching them, sizing them up, she thought, and she returned his gaze. Apparently coming to a decision, he nodded, and sat forward in his chair, hands clasped together.

"Gateway is neutral. It always has been and must remain that way, if we are to maintain our status. This is a safe place, for all races, all people. However, here, in the safety of my inner sanctuary, safe from even the most gifted of spirituals, I have no qualms admitting that I detest the Atrile and everything they stand for."

She nodded at him, working hard to keep the smile from her face.

"Thanks, that means a lot."

He nodded back, flicking a hand at the world beyond his office.

"I'm not the only one either, there are many out there would gladly see the Atrile brought low. Word from the Nexus is that you've already managed that, so my money's on it happening again."

She got a flash then, of the reality that this man lived alone and bored, crying out for some sort of entertainment, something to liven up his existence. She had him on a pedestal, the owner of one of the biggest space stations in the galaxy, a man of power and intrigue. But in reality, his power, his station, was his prison. It seemed that for all the exotic and wonderful things they had seen so far, there was plenty of repetition also. He leaned forward, voice dropping.

"I cannot help you, not overtly, but I can refill your life support, fuel, guns and anything else you need, and I can offer you full lodging for your stay here. I can also offer you one piece of advice—"

He was interrupted by a knocking on the door, followed immediately by it opening, admitting a tall woman, with dark blue skin, up-swept ears, wearing a suit that was similar to his. He looked annoyed for a moment, then saw the look on her face, and stood up.

"Sir, I'm sorry to disturb you, but I thought you would want to know. We have spotted a number of humans on board."

Ally, trying not to eavesdrop, but having little choice, swung round in her chair and stared at the woman.

"Why is that so important?" She blurted out. The captain gave her a slightly disdainful glance, then turned back to his aide.

"Definitely slaves?"

She nodded.

"Dammit. And the Atrile?"

"They're still here, and the Homeships aren't moving yet, but it's unlikely to be long."

'Are the regulars ready?"

She shook her head, flushing. 'They won't fight the Atrile, sir, I'm sorry.'

The captain bit his lip, staring past her at the wall. Ally waited for him to shout, but he took a deep breath, and his voice remained soft.

"So who do we have?

"Almost no one. It's been peaceful for such a long time..."

She spread her hands, forehead furrowed in thought.

"We should have Feril, he never goes anywhere. And possibly Neve. That's it."

"Dammit." He slammed his fist into his palm. Ally, who had watched the exchange entirely baffled, and smarting from the look he had given her, couldn't keep quiet any longer.

"Sorry, I still don't get what the problem is?"

Both of them looked at her this time, then the woman took pity, shaking her head as she spoke.

"The Atrile never do the dirty work, why would they when they have an unlimited number of slaves to do it for them? Any time you see a group of humans anywhere, it means the Atrile need something doing, something that involves violence or piracy."

"So you're saying, when most people see a human, they expect them to kill or rob somebody?"

The aide had the grace to look sheepish as she nodded. Ally realised the captain was speaking urgently into his comms. When he straightened up, he looked straight at Ally, though spoke to his aide.

"We have Feril and Neve. He's already up and running, she'll be ready in a few minutes. I want you to stay here and monitor, keep me informed. Ally, Stem, I think it best you head back to the room your friend keeps, and stay there. I've already ordered your ships to be fitted and they should be ready soon. It may be necessary for you to leave soon, but I'm hoping it doesn't come to that. I'll let you know."

He was already heading out the door and she scrambled up, Stem one step ahead as they chased him to the lift. She had a moment to glance upward, this time catching sight of the horribly familiar shape of a Homeship moving slowly above the station, and the view that had seemed glorious and expansive was suddenly claustrophobic. They jumped into the lift and she turned to the Captain.

"Is it really as bad as you think?"

He was surprised when he turned to her.

"Of all those here, I would have thought you were the last person who needed to ask that. They are slaves, Ally, entirely controlled by the Atrile. They will do anything they are ordered, regardless of how it impacts others, or even themselves."

He stopped for a moment, thinking, then continued.

'What you did on the Nexus was brave, impressive, but in the long run, humans are still trouble, still viewed with suspicion, and rightly so.'

She gritted her teeth, waving a hand to shut him up, but he went right on talking. 'This isn't your fault, what's happening here. Or what happens elsewhere. You, at least, are trying to make a difference.'

It was nice of him to say it, but it didn't stop her lip from curling. She was making a difference, but it would mean nothing if everyone else still hated them. She stalked away from the lift as the doors slid open, and down the platform toward Bridyant's room. She longed to clamber back into bed, and wait for someone else to clean up the mess, but as she entered the room, she stopped, hand over her mouth.

Every piece of furniture was destroyed, overturned and ripped apart. The drinks booth was wrecked also, and the artwork that had lined the walls was smashed across the floor. There was no sign of Bridyant, or the others.

Chapter 17

She ran into the first sleep room, and found it in the same state, the mattress turned onto the floor and the frame ripped from the wall. She met Stem back in the main room, and they stood, frozen for a moment, amidst the carnage.

"What were they looking for?"

She turned to look at him, shrugging. "I don't think they were looking for anything, except us."

"Why?"

He gestured to the room, and she shrugged again. Like he needed to ask. They were human, weren't they? That was reason enough, apparently. She stepped out of the door and made her way back toward the lift, Stem running out just after her. He grabbed her sleeve.

"The captain said we should stay here. Now that they've already been, assuming it was the slaves, it's gonna be pretty safe."

She touched his hand, letting him get a wave of the rage that was threatening to overwhelm her, and he stopped, grabbing her hand to pull her back.

"Ally, stop for a minute. I get you're pissed, I am too, but what are we supposed to do?"

She looked at him, her forehead creased.

"Don't you think we ought to help Bridyant, to help the others who have promised to help us?"

He looked down at his feet, then back at her, his face twisted.

"I know, I know, I just... I want to get to Earth. It feels like every time we try, something else gets in the way. If we go and get shot, we never get there, you know?"

She looked over his shoulder, down across Gateway, at the thousands milling, going about lives she couldn't even imagine. Then she looked back at him, and felt her heart lurch, a sick feeling swelling up. She shoved it down, refusing to even look at what it meant.

"But what good is getting to Earth, and freeing the human race, if we leave behind us people who we actually know, who have actually made an effort? They matter more to me, right now, than those we don't know."

She saw his face crease in confusion and reached out a hand.

"I wanna go to Earth, you know that, and we have to use the spell, and get rid of the Atrile, of course, but Atan and the others matter. I'm not gonna hide whilst they're getting attacked."

She turned away, ignoring the burning in her gut and stomped to the lift, not wanting to turn and see whether he was following. She was thirty feet away from the lift, when the doors slid open, and three humans stepped out. They were dressed in the same dark uniforms as those on their Homeship had been, and carried the same blasters.

She was frozen, staring at them. All three raised their weapons and fired. Her face hit the floor, her teeth slamming together, and she grunted as the air rushed from her lungs. Stem rolled away from her and came up running, heading straight for the humans, shouting as he went. She struggled to her feet, screaming at him to stop, then a light blinded her and she covered her eyes.

She could hear the humans screaming, horrible, pain-filled howling, and she opened her eyes again, fearing what she would see. Stem was a little way ahead, also on his knees. In front of them, the three humans were staggering about, covered in flames - hair frying, skin melting. She turned away, one hand over her mouth as her gorge rose.

Balanced on the rail was the most extraordinary being she had seen since the Nexus. She was short, five foot tops, but supported by an enormous set of wings, flapping gently. Her hands gripped a cannon, flames trickling slowly out the front. Behind her, the screaming was dying down, becoming low moans and she turned back. They were on the floor now, humps of flaming flesh, the clothes burned away. The stench was sweet and cloying, and made her want to vomit even harder.

Her mind rebelled as well as her stomach, the relief she felt warring with the sheer wrongness of what had just happened. How could she feel anything other than revulsion? But without the help, she and Stem would be dead.

She turned quickly away, and back to the woman, who was settling onto the platform. Ally stood up and approached her, and was greeted with the cannon. She stopped, putting her hands up, talking quickly.

"Hey, it's fine, I'm with you. I mean, if you killed those guys, then I guess I'm with you. I'm Ally...?"

The woman let the gun drop, stepping forward with a hand outstretched. They shook and she smiled, showing two rows of teeth, neatly filed to sharp points. Ally stared for a moment, then smiled weakly back.

"Neve. This is your fault, I believe?"

"Uhh, well, ah, yeah, I guess so, though, you know, they started it."

Neve smiled again, this time with a little more humour.

"Yes they did. I have to go hunt. You might want to arm yourselves."

"Where? Where can we get guns?"

Neve stared at her for a moment, then flapped her wings, drifting slowly over to the lift. Around the corner from it, she tapped a long string of numbers into a panel and it slid aside, revealing a cubby. Within were a set of blasters, extra cartridges, and thick body jackets. Neve pulled out two of everything and handed them over, then, without another word, ran to the edge of the platform, and threw herself off.

She sailed upward, eyes staring down at the platforms. Standing next to one another, Ally and Stem watched her go, wide eyed, then Ally turned to Stem.

"You won't see that on Earth."

He looked away from her and busied himself putting his jacket on. She sighed and did the same, then they entered the lift and headed down. Stem thought they should try the platform Bridyant had taken him to the first time they had come here, and short of a better option, that was where they headed.

As they emerged from the lift, a number of the travellers saw the guns and moved quickly away, a few piling into the lift they had just evacuated. They had taken only a couple of steps, when two men, sat nearby, rose out of their seats, brought weapons to bear, and fired across the busy platform. She was ready this time and threw herself to the ground, Stem beside her. The lift shaft behind them absorbed the bolts, slivers of steel flying in all directions. The others on the platform reacted in all sorts of way, some screaming and hitting the floor, others running, some merely sipping their drinks and settling back for the show.

She saw all this in the split second she lay flat, then she came up to her knees. She sighted the human slaves and aimed her blaster. The first shot went wide and she watched it travel across the hall, slamming into the far wall. She winced, and another blast of gun fire sent her back to the ground. She rolled onto her side, looking at Stem.

"What do we do?"

He raised his eyebrows, then the gun, and indicated he was about to stand. She went with him and they both fired at the humans. She didn't hit either, but she was getting closer. Stem caught one in the chest, and sent him flying backward, crashing through chairs. The other didn't react at all to his mate being shot and instead stayed standing, and kept shooting. She dropped to her knees, resting her arms against the table she hid behind, steadying her aim.

She squeezed the trigger, one eye closed, and felt a weird sensation go through her, a shaking in her limbs that was part adrenaline, part sickness. The human she had shot tumbled back, a smoking hole in his face, and she stood, running over to the bodies. They were both dead, lying still and she stared at their faces, desperately thankful that she didn't recognise them. Stem joined her and she took his hand, pleased to find her shaking mirrored in him.

She heard a shout and spun around, bringing her gun up. Atan stood on the far side of the platform, waving madly at them, and she gasped, then lowered her gun and ran over to him.

"Hey, are you OK?"

He nodded, his usual smile conspicuous by its absence.

"Yes, fortunately, Lucid and I were still out in the station when the room was attacked. As far as I know, there was no one there at the time, for which we can be most grateful."

He looked at their guns, then sighed and shook his head. She felt oddly guilty, and found herself excusing the weaponry.

"We met someone, a lady called Neve. I think the captain got her to help, she gave us the guns."

"Ahh."

A pause.

"So sad that it must come to this, but then, it almost always does. How did your meeting with the captain go?"

She nodded, smiling, and filled him in, by the end of which he, too, was grinning.

"Well, that's rather grand, isn't it?"

They were sat a table, but the sound of gunfire pulled her from her seat and across to the edge of the platform, joined by others rushing across. Looking down, they watched three humans on the platform below, ducking and dodging their way through the crowds in pursuit of a tall, thin man, who had come with them from Station Nephal. Ally pointed her gun over the balcony, then pulled it back.

"Damn, there's far too many people, I don't have a hope."

Atan was looking at her, one eyebrow raised, and she shook her head, exclaiming in a loud voice.

"What? What should I do?"

"You are allowing yourself to be led by what is around you. How else could you fight those below?"

She stared into his eyes, then it clicked and she lowered her's, face blushing bright red. She sat, and floated free of her body, then hurtled down to the platform. The first human she found was kneeling behind a tipped up table, taking lazy shots over the top, sometimes hitting nothing, other times hitting innocents. She couldn't believe that this was what most people saw of humans, this mindless violence propagated by the Atrile in their callous use of them.

She dived into his mind, recoiling as she hit a thick web of the same strange substance that had cloaked all of their minds on the Homeship. This time, though, it was much thicker, and stronger, and she dug her fingers in, pulling with all her might. It wouldn't give and she backed off, before trying a different approach.

She laid her hands against the sticky mass, and imagined it becoming hard and brittle. Slowly, beneath her fingers, the stickiness faded and the substance stopped moving. Letting go, she rapped her knuckles against it, then punched it hard. It shattered, falling away in pieces, and she was left with a brain that looked withered and dark, the natural colours dulled.

She sank in, and felt tears spring up in her eyes. There was nothing here, the normal memories and feelings and beliefs, just shadows, drifting aimlessly down empty corridors. What had happened? The humans they'd freed on the Homeship hadn't been like this. It was as if someone had emptied their minds, taken away everything that made them real.

She almost ran, rushing back to her body to hide, but now wasn't the time. And it made it easier for her to do what she had to, and for that, she was grateful.

Something clicked, and she realised that he had gone still, frozen in place. She tried to raise the arms and they came up smoothly. In his brain, she smiled to herself, then lifted the gun and turned. His comrade was crouched a few metres away behind a table, and she aimed and fired. The blast was close, and he was lifted from his feet and went flying through the chairs with a crash.

The third human looked across, face creased in confusion, and she made the body stand, getting closer. The man watched her as she came, still confused, but still not understanding what was happening. When she was close enough to be sure she wouldn't miss, she raised her gun and put a blast through his chest.

She glanced up, to see Atan's and Stem's faces amongst those peering down from the platform, and they clapped, Stem giving her the thumbs up. She left the body and flew upward. Below her, the brain-dead man collapsed in a heap, limbs floppy and awkward.

She opened her eyes, feeling the need to drink a lot of water, and possibly have a shower as soon as she got the chance. She put her hands on her knees, taking deep breaths, and going back in her mind to the dull, lifeless brain. There had been nothing there, nothing left of the human person, she had done only what she had to. She stood up and they pushed through the watching crowd to the escalator. Down to the next floor and they met up with the tall man, called Javin.

She was happy to pass her blaster to him, and could tell just by the way he hefted it, that he was far more proficient than she was ever going to be. The four of them gathered in a circle, planning their next move. Javin was all for carrying on down, killing as they went. She and Atan favoured a more introspective route, the two of them scouting on the spiritual, and intervening when someone was in danger. Stem was happy to stay and guard their empty bodies, so Javin opted to stay with him.

They found a secluded corner and she and Atan floated free, the other two stood in front of them, guns at the ready. They had traveled no further than the next platform down, when a familiar voice crawled its way in.

"Hello, Ally, we were hoping you'd join us here, we have a small matter of revenge to discuss with you."

Around the corner walked three of the tall, green-skinned men she had fought in the Nexus. They were carrying guns, and before she had time to react, they fired.

Chapter 18

She hurtled upward, far faster than the blasts headed toward them, Atan keeping pace. The three men came rushing up to meet them, guns firing, and she reversed direction, flying down past them. This time, however, Atan failed to keep up, and a bolt caught him in the leg, sending him spinning out across the hall.

With a roar, she charged at the nearest Atrile, a knife appearing in her hand as she went. He barely had time to turn before she plunged it into his side, then pulled it free and stuck it through his neck. His eyes widened and he vanished, leaving traces of blood floating in the air. She stared at it, seeing through the liquid, to another of them sighting down the barrel, ready to fire.

It happened in a split second, another of those realisations that it didn't have to work like this. She put a hand out, feeling the energy that rushed toward her, and she changed it, though she didn't know how, transforming the heat to light. A bright burst of white filled the space between them and she covered her eyes, blinking furiously as it faded.

She recovered quicker than her enemies and was through the light, grabbing the gun from the shooter's hand and changing it, twisting the metal until it was sharp. She thrust it into the Atrile's chest, shoving him back and he flew across the hall, and out through the side wall.

The third was watching her, eyes narrowed, gun at the ready. She gave him a 'come on' gesture, and was rewarded by a snarl and a shot. This she imagined as a flock of birds and tiny, spirit creatures flapped and flew around the hall. Some of the onlookers had realised what was happening and more people were appearing on the spirit plane, watching.

With a hiss, the Atrile vanished, and she spun, searching for Atan. He was nowhere to be seen and she rushed back to her body, finding him sitting up and cradling his leg. A vicious burn had appeared covering everything from the foot to the knee and she touched it gently, feeling the tight, papery skin. He winced, looking at her with wide eyes.

"I knew you had power, but that was really rather impressive. You can manipulate objects, and the environment. I have genuinely found only one other that can do that, and you've already met him."

He clapped his hands together, his smile back in its rightful place. She blushed, looking at her hands, then stood and stared out over the station.

"What now?"

"I think it would behove us to continue our search. The Atrile may have left but their soldiers are still here, however many of them there are. To pinch a particularly human phrase, we aren't out of the woods yet."

He slipped free of his body before she had time to argue, and she sat back down, nodding to Stem before joining Atan. Back on the spiritual plane, his leg looked just as bad, but he seemed immune to the pain, or at least very good at ignoring it.

They went more quickly now, charging from platform to platform, finding no sign of the slaves. It was the noise that alerted them to the fighting, the sound of swords clashing together, and they came to a huge platform, covered in chairs, sofas and dining tables. Running between them, and over them, were Lucid and a man who looked remarkably similar in everything but dress. The man wore a uniform, like that of the captain, and Neve. Perhaps this was Feril?

The two of them were brandishing swords, fighting a running battle with eight of the humans, all armed the same way. Where the hell had Lucid found swords? And how had he convinced the humans to do the same? She shook her head, moving nearer the fighting. She caught sight of Lucid, and saw the fierce grin plastered across his features, and heard the shout that accompanied every thrust or parry he made.

She watched with amazement as he ran backwards, parrying the furious thrust of his opponent, then jumped back and up onto a table, taking it off its legs and riding it to the ground, now using it as a barrier. The human ran into it, slicing with his sword, and Lucid stepped neatly out of the way, then back in close, his blade sliding over the top of the table and deep into his opponent's chest.

Pulling his blade free, he shouted in triumph and turned just in time to parry another blow, sending his attacker sprawling past him. He spun and circled the hapless human, taunting him with mock attacks. The man ran at him, swiping the air, and he danced back once again. He stopped suddenly, one hand on the back of a chair, and when the man attacked again, he swung the chair, smashing it against both the sword and his opponent's hand, sending the blade spinning away. Bringing the chair back across his face, he knocked his attacker to his knees, then put his blade through his throat, tearing out the veins and windpipe with his back thrust. The man dropped, face down to the floor, and Lucid turned once more to the fray.

Ally had been frozen for the few seconds in which the entire thing occured, watching, astounded and distracted by the casual skill, but now she floated down into the mind of one of humans, removing the coating and slipping into it. It felt like putting on wet clothes. She made him walk, jerky movements, and take his sword out as he headed for his comrades. He and two others had been holding back, waiting for the right time to strike, and she managed to stick the sword through the nearest one's ear before he realised anything was going on.

He collapsed to the floor, tearing the blade from her hands, and she stepped back, hands up. The other human, eyes eerily blank, drew his own sword and came at her. With a scream, she leapt free of the body, just as the blade dug into its belly. She felt the first sting of the iron and shivered as she hovered just above the corpse. She had no idea what would happen if she was in a body that got killed, but just the touch of the blade made her certain it would be bad.

The distraction had given the man she assumed was Feril time to sneak up, and he stepped in close behind the human, and drew a long bladed dagger across his throat. As he toppled, Feril sat and came free of his body, drifting up to where Ally hovered.

"You would be Ally, I presume."

She giggled. He sounded just the same as Lucid, bored and slightly superior, and she nodded. He gestured to the dead men lying beneath them.

"That was a good trick, whatever you did, thank you."

"Hey, no problem. Are you Feril? And, like, you're the same race as Lucid, right?"

He nodded, face breaking into what she had already decided was a rare grin.

"Indeed. It is nice to meet another Larlien, particularly a master thief. They are rare these days. You keep interesting company..."

"Yeah, I'm just getting that. Where did you find the swords?'

He smiled. 'There is a stall, on the ground floor, of which Lucid was more than happy to avail himself. It is actually forbidden to carry projectile weapons aboard, and these humans didn't make it through the security. The regulars manned up for that one, at least.'

She nodded, not sure what to make of the sneer in his voice. 'Have you seen any of the others?"

"If, by others, you are referring to those you came in with, then yes. Three of them left the station late last night, without any apparent intention to return. That leaves eight, by my count."

"Yeah, so we've got two of them, Atan and Javin, so there's six left."

"You seem concerned that they may have difficulty in looking after themselves?"

He paused, turning to watch as Lucid ran down the last human, jumping from a table to land with both feet in his back, driving him to the ground. As he fell, his face caught the edge of a chair and snapped his head back. She winced as Lucid jammed his sword through the back of the poor man's neck, then wrenched it out. He turned back to Ally, with a sardonic smile.

"They may not all be quite as capable as my countryman, but I imagine you can rely on them to deal with a human or two."

Her face flushed, and she nodded.

"Uh, yeah, right, I just didn't want them thinking I'd abandoned them, that's all."

He smiled more kindly at her, and nodded approvingly. How was it everyone could make her feel stupid, even when she had the gift? She shot upward, suddenly realising that Atan wasn't there. She stared across the hall, but there were hundreds of travelers now on the spiritual plane, flying around, searching for who knew what. Her, probably, which couldn't be good. She rushed back up to where Stem and Javin were waiting, slipping into her body, and opening her eyes.

Stem's face was inches from hers, his finger on her lips, and she stayed right where she was. He crept slowly sideways until she could see past him, to where a large group of humans had just emerged from the lift and were spreading out across the platform. Ally and the others were tucked near the back, down the side of the lift, and she bit her lip as she pulled the knife from her belt. She looked longingly at the gun in Javin's hand, then up again at the humans. Perhaps she could strike first without them knowing.

She closed her eyes and slipped out, settling slowly into the mind of the human nearest them, just now leaving the lift. She hardened and cracked away the slave substance, then took control of the body, shivering as she again encountered the empty mind. It was becoming easier each time she did it, and she could move him with very little effort, his movements almost smooth. This needed to be quick and, ideally, draw them away from their hiding place.

She experimented with moving the mouth, and understood very quickly that it wasn't going to work. Instead she burrowed into the brain, that dirty feeling coming on strong again, and she had to work hard to keep going until she found the bit that made words. Everything she did came naturally, even though she was making it up. Kind of like kissing for the first time. That was not a good comparison.

Satisfied that she had control, she broke into a run, instructing the brain at the same time.

"Over there, there they are!"

He shouted, running past his comrades and across the platform. They scattered, charging after him, and she grinned. Most of the way to the railing, she spun, bringing the gun up, and started to fire, unloading shot after shot into the approaching human slaves. The need to vomit and the hatred she felt for the Atrile battled within her for superiority, but she kept squeezing the trigger until one of them had the wherewithal to shoot back, and she jumped out, leaving the body to sag, then twitch and jerk as the bullets found their mark. She hovered above the carnage, not wanting to look but unable to leave without checking what she'd done. Six were down, horrible gaping wounds smoking on prone bodies.

She dropped back in to her body, and opened her eyes, seeing Javin already sprinting across the platform, Stem following more cautiously. Javin began to fire, taking three down before they realised they were being shot at, and the remaining humans scattered, diving for cover.

Ally was deliberating whether she should leave her and Atan's body unguarded, when Neve came soaring in from above, a ball of fire sweeping across the humans. Four of them came running from their shelter, screaming as flames caught skin and hair. The other two seemed to have escaped, but on her second pass she caught them both, and then landed, stepping daintily between the dead bodies and the screaming torches. She walked between Javin and Stem, and came over.

"We have most of them, I think. You certainly did a good enough job here, though. The captain would like to see you, if you can spare the time."

She said it in such a way that Ally knew Neve had added the last bit on herself. She nodded, motioning to Atan.

"As soon as he returns, we'll head straight up there, and, you know, thanks again."

Neve nodded, then took off, swooping away between the platforms.

Chapter 19

Atan didn't return. Lucid and Feril appeared a few minutes after Neve flew off, followed shortly by the others. They had all had confrontations, but come through unscathed. Ally checked Atan's body every minute to ensure there was a pulse, and spent the rest of the time pacing back and forth.

Bridyant was also missing, and she was even more worried about her. They had last seen her in the room, when they went to meet the captain, and though they had found no blood, they had no way of knowing whether she had been there when the slaves trashed it. Her head throbbed, forehead scrunched in a permanent frown. She paused in her pacing, rubbing her temples with her fingers, squeezing her eyes closed in an effort to relax.

Stem came up behind her, putting his arms around her waist and giving her a squeeze.

"He's gonna come back, so's Bridyant, don't worry."

She sighed, leaning back into his embrace for a moment, then turned to face him.

"You sure, I mean, really sure?"

He nodded, confident, and she hugged him, a little of the tension easing from her. She broke away, then walked over to Lucid.

"We need to go and see the captain. Will you make sure Atan's ok, please?"

He nodded, and she gave the prone body one more glance before heading for the lift. They came out under the stars, and she felt her spirits rise a little as she gazed up at the amazing sight. They walked to the captain's office, finding the door open, and went inside.

He was sat at his desk, brow furrowed, eyes fixed on a screen as he jabbed at the buttons before him with one finger. He waved absently as they came in, and they sat down, waiting. He had a remarkably expressive face and she began imagining what he was looking at, inventing a complex story to go with his every frown and raise of the eyebrows. After a few minutes, he looked up at them, and sounded harrassed.

"The Atrile haven't left, which I find quite surprising. The humans are clearly from their Homeship, which means they have violated the ruling I set out. By rights, I could destroy their ships and no one would bat an eyelid. That they haven't vanished gives me cause to think they have something up whatever it is they count as a sleeve, and that is unlikely to be good."

He stared at them, and she realised he was waiting for an explanation. She shrugged, feeling suddenly guilty.

"I, um, we don't know."

She glanced at Stem, looking for support.

"Um, we fought the humans, fought back, I mean, because they destroyed Bridyant's rooms. Also, Neve gave us the guns, so I guess we thought that made it alright."

He waved her to quiet.

"That's fine, no problem at all, it was clearly self-defence. Is that all that you've done?"

She nodded earnestly, the prone body of Atan flashing through her mind. She hesitated, and looked at him again. She still didn't want to trust him, but he seemed on the level. She let her head rock back, staring up at the ceiling, then took a deep breath.

"There are two we still haven't found. Bridyant and Atan. Atan's on the spiritual plane, but I don't know where Bridyant is. She was in the room when we came to find you, so she may have been captured by the slaves, but I don't know."

The captain stared at her levelly, then raised an eyebrow.

"How likely is it that either of those people have done something foolish?"

She snorted, then saw that he was being entirely serious.

"Sorry, what do you mean by foolish?"

"Any act of aggression against the Atrile would give them cause to retaliate."

He sighed, setting his elbows on the edge of the desk.

"There is no law here, no governing body to make the decisions. I am an independent business man who keeps the peace using hired soldiers. It isn't difficult, because I cater exceptionally well for the needs of my customers. I may have the external firepower to hurt the Atrile very seriously, but if they decide they want Gateway for themselves, and can bring enough humans on board, it would be a very difficult fight to win."

Her eyes were wide, and she glanced over her shoulder, then back to him. Stem's face had gone white. The captain stood, and began pacing, keeping himself in check only through force of will, his lips bitten hard between his teeth.

'They must have a reason for being here, and being this persistent. What do they want from you?'

She shook her head. 'They don't want anything from me, they just want revenge.'

The captain hissed, and thumped the desk, standing. 'That still doesn't explain why they're still here. They won't get revenge, not whilst you're under my protection, unless they have something they can use as a reason to stay.

Ally squirmed, then shook her head, her face getting hot. She stood, getting to his level.

"No, I'm sorry, but I don't believe that Bridyant or Atan would have done anything stupid, they just wouldn't."

They stared at one another, then he nodded slightly, and sat down.

"If that's the case, then why are they still here?

Stem spoke up, his voice low and shaky.

"They could just be waiting for us to leave."

They both turned to him, Ally feeling a shiver run down her back. She nodded, and turned back to the captain.

"They can just wait until we leave, then chase us down. The Homeship can outrun anything we've got, no problem."

She sat down, her gut clenching, and reached out a hand that Stem grabbed. The captain was swaying his head from side to side, pushing his chair back so he balanced on the back legs.

"You may be right."

He paused.

"There isn't much I can do for you if they are. Once you're off the station, my jurisdiction is over."

He spread his hands apart.

"Sorry folks, I just can't get involved out there, not with a race as powerful as them."

She nodded. He had been more than fair as it was. His voice cut through her thoughts.

"Of course, we still don't know that for sure. We need to find your people, and the sooner the better. If I can help, let me know."

He turned back to his desk, and she took that to mean they were dismissed. She stood, pulling Stem up, and turned to the door. They left, walking back to the lift. She realised her fist was clenched, her nails digging into her palms, and she was squeezing Stem's hand so hard the bones were grinding. He stopped abruptly, pulling her back to stand in front of him.

"What do we do?"

She laughed humorlessly, eyes turning up to the freedom that waited above them.

"What do you think?"

"We could just go, just the two of us. They may not even notice, and if they did, then at least none of the others would be in danger."

She wanted to punch him. He'd never been a coward, never been scared until the Nexus, now all he seemed to think about was himself. She checked herself. That wasn't fair, he thought about her as well, and he had every right to be scared. It all just felt so small now. He had been the one with the big plans, the dreams of freedom that had galvanised them into action, but somehow he was getting smaller, getting further away, while she was believing more every day.

She sighed, and looked up again, felt them calling to her. She turned to him and shook her head.

"It would never work; they know me, remember, they'll be waiting. As soon as we leave, they'll be all over us. We need, somehow, to get rid of them before we go anywhere."

Stem's eyes lit up and he held his hands out as if he were cupping a ball between them.

"OK, so, the captain has said that he has the fire power, right, that he could cause them serious damage, enough to get rid of them."

She nodded.

"So, all we have to do is convince him to use it, or, I guess, use it ourselves."

She raised her eyebrows. The things she had been thinking only moments ago seemed suddenly petty, and she flushed, nodding more, her mind beginning to race.

"You're a genius, yeah, that's it."

Then she stopped, her smile dropping.

'Those ships are filled with humans, no different from you or dad.'

He shook his head. 'Didn't you say their brains were gone, emptied out or something?

'The ones who attacked here were, but that doesn't mean they all are.' She paused, and shook her head. I don't know, I just... We have to find Bridyant and Atan first, find out where they've gone. We can't risk doing anything until they're safe. Then we can think about it."

He nodded, the scared look gone from his face. She rested her hand against his cheek, then kissed him. He looked surprised, then grinned and kissed her back. As one, they turned and entered the lift.

They arrived back on the platform just in time to see Atan blink slowly, then open his eyes and stretch. He saw them and waved, sketching a rough smile that she could tell, even from some distance away, was lacking the usual power. By the time they got to him, he was up and talking to Lucid.

Both of them turned when they walked up, faces grim, as Atan broke the news.

"They have Bridyant. I'm terribly sorry."

Ally swore, drawing surprised glances from the others, then she bit her lip and nodded for him to continue.

"I followed them on-board. I can be remarkably subtle when I choose. It's a strange place, isn't it? I know where she's being kept."

"What took you so long?"

He sighed, a huge event that suggested the ends of worlds and worse.

"It's a dead place, Ally, it must have been frightful for you. No one even knows the spiritual plane exists, let alone uses it. Unfortunately, it means that anyone there in spirit is rather conspicuous. No, no, they didn't spot me. Like I said, I can be sneaky when the occasion demands it. But it meant hiding for some considerable time, until the two Atrile on board came back onto the Station."

Ally let out a breath. Atan was back and safe, but the sickness in her stomach wasn't going away.

Bridyant was captured, and on a Homeship, which meant that she was going to have to go back on board a Homeship, and that was the last thing she'd ever intended to do. She updated them with Stem's escape plan, then they fell to planning how they were going to rescue Bridyant.

"The entire thing might be a plan to get you back on board, you can't go, Ally."

Stem was probably right, but she didn't want to hear it. She couldn't force him to go, knowing how he felt about the Atrile, but was pleasantly surprised when he made it very clear he intended to go as well. Atan would be the guide, and Lucid supplied the sword.

As the four of them made their way down to the floor of the hall, another thought struck her.

'Atan, when you were on board. Did you notice anything about the humans? Were they... normal?'

The rotund alien stopped, and gave her an odd look. 'I confess I have little experience, besides the two of you, but you are far from normal.' He hesitated, bashful for a moment. 'They were, empty, for want of a better word. I came across a number who were simply sitting, staring at nothing, as though someone had switched them off.' He looked from one to the other. 'Is that normal?'

Stem gave her a look and she shook her head. 'No, it's not. We think something's happened to them, like the Atrile have brain-wiped them or something?'

Atan's face clouded over, and she watched in surprise as he gritted his teeth. He nodded slowly. 'It is possible, especially for a race as powerful as the Atrile. We will investigate further, once we are on board.'

She nodded, going cold as another thought struck her. She tugged on Stem's sleeve, muttering to him. 'Do you think they did it because of us, because of what we did?'

The look on his face was answer enough, and she moaned, low in her throat. She put her hands over her face, rubbing it furiously, as though she could somehow scrub away the pain. Stem touched her shoulder. She kept her eyes screwed shut, then relented and looked at him.

'Look, it's just a thought, but...'

He trailed off and she nudged him.

"Yeah?"

"Well, I thought, why don't you go in there on the spiritual plane and just kick ass, like you did on the Nexus?"

Atan turned to watch her as she answered. She managed to restrain the tears that threatened to burst free, and resist the urge to curl up where she was, and bury her head. She bit her lip.

'I can't, I just...' She shook her head. 'I'm still making it up. They've destroyed the minds of thousands of humans and I'm still figuring it out as a I go. I'm sorry, I just can't.'

Atan stepped forward.

'We could do it together, we—'

'NO. No, you've already done enough, please, let's just go find Bridyant.'

Her eyes were wet and she scrubbed her face again. Stem put his arm on her shoulders.

"Hey, it's fine, really, and I'm glad you aren't doing it. I just wanted to check."

She gave him a grateful smile, then the tunnel lay before them, heading away toward the larger docks. They walked into it and the walls and ceilings closed around them, the corridor feeling narrow and cramped after the expanse of the hall. There were a number of cruisers here, massive vessels carrying cargo, or passengers, but only a couple came close to the size of the Homeships. All four were docked at the far end of the gantry, away from everything else, and the walk took long enough for her stomach to start churning and her head to think of every way this could go wrong.

Atan stopped them, a little way from the end, putting one hand to his lips. They crowded around as he muttered.

"You will need to guard your mind. If they are on the spiritual, they will spot you, no doubts at all."

He paused for a moment, staring into space.

"Try to imagine a wall around your brain, but not one made of steel, or stone. It needs to be reflective, something that shows the watcher themselves.

Steel, they will notice, but seeing themselves, they will think us just as everyone else on board, a slave."

She nodded and built one inside, sliding panels together until they fit seamlessly, and everything she was, was hidden safe behind the mirror. She looked at Stem and he nodded. His face was pale, hands shaking. She gave him a smile and he tried, and failed, to return it, then clenched his hands together, and turned to the end of the gantry.

They sneaked up to the entry and peered in, seeing the docking bridge, and the hanger beyond, a sight that was so familiar, she felt a twinge of home-sickness. She could picture Dad standing in there, holding his tools, thumping the side of the Vale, and her eyes grew wet. She blinked it away, stepped onto the bridge, and crept up it, working hard to stop her boots from clanging against the metal.

She reached the hanger and slipped out, stepping swiftly back into the shadows. The others followed, equally quiet, and just like that, they were back on a Homeship, where it had all begun. She realised she was holding her breath, and let it out slowly. She stared across the hanger, as the door in the far wall slid open, and her breathing stopped completely as one of the Atrile stepped through.

Chapter 20

She froze, back pressed hard against the hanger wall, eyes glued to the creature as it made its slow way into the hanger. It was flanked by a number of slaves, all wearing the same, dark uniforms and carrying guns.

She let her breath out and it sounded loud in the hanger, so loud she winced, a hand clapped over her mouth. She glanced at the others. Atan and Lucid were pressed flat, faces calm and eyes wary. Stem was trying to climb backward through the wall, face white and hands held up in front of him. His mouth was moving, no sounds coming out, and she tried to catch his eye, blinking furiously, but to no avail.

The Atrile came closer, heading for the docking bridge. If she moved to grab Stem, it would see them, or the humans around it would. But if he made a sound, the outcome would be the same. She longed to go onto the spiritual plane, to calm him that way, but even the slightest hint and the creature would be on her in a second.

She bit her lip, a trickle of blood running into her mouth, as it came closer, and closer. She could see the folds of flesh, the green tumescence that made her feel sick as it rolled and slid in time with its steps. She clenched her fists, dizzy from the lack of air, each breath a tiny snatch of oxygen that barely touched her lungs. Stem's entire body was shaking, and she could see the line of sweat that ran down his temple.

It passed, and she caught its smell, a strange tang of oranges left in the sun a little too long. Then it disappeared into the bridge, followed by its attendant slaves. She listened to the scrape of its feet as it moved, ever so slowly, down and into the gantry.

They stayed motionless until the sound of the slaves' boots on the gantry floor faded away, then she gasped, sucking in huge lungfuls of air. Stem slid down the wall, his eyes still wide, his hands clutching his knees. She knelt beside him, wrapping her arms around his head, feeling his entire body shake. She tried to calm him, but where she had a wall of mirrors, his entire being was wrapped inside a ball, no gaps anywhere. It was, she reflected, rather impressive, and she smiled as she rested her head against his messy hair.

Finally, she stood, exchanging looks with the other two, who were both grinning. Atan's voice was unusually quiet.

"Well, that was rather exciting, wasn't it? Shall we?"

He gestured to the hanger door and they scampered across the open space and into the Homeship. The familiar rounded corridors brought back more memories, of Dad and the last few weeks they had spent here, when they had become free. She had no idea whether this was their ship, or a different one, there was no apparent difference. The routes from the hanger were known to them, the paths like coming home.

The corridors were almost deserted, the occasional person passing them quietly, eyes downcast. Every time they spotted someone, her heart began to race and she gripped her gun, but they always went without comment, their docile minds unquestioning. Had she ever been so lost? She didn't think so, but it was difficult to remember, everything before the discovery was hazy, fragments of events. She had some stuff, certain things, like learning to fly, that were crystal, and she could see as clear as day, but everything else, the day to day stuff, was gone.

She stopped the others, leaned against Stem, and slipped free of her body. She floated down the tunnel until she found one of the humans, and then drifted down into his mind. She sank through the coating, and found beneath it the same flat emptiness of those that had attacked them on Gateway.

She tore herself free, screaming silently as she hurtled back to her body.

She stayed where she was, the pressure of Stem's hands keeping her together, keeping her sane. It wasn't her fault, no more than any of this was. If only she truly believed that. She nodded to the others, confirming what she'd found, and they continued on, subdued and round shouldered.

The lift waited for them, and they exchanged glances before stepping in. She could still see the Lord, splattered and strewn across the floor, and a smile reached her lips. It felt wrong to rejoice in the death of anything, but it was the freedom that accompanied it that made her happy. She had never really tried to fathom the motivation behind the creatures that had enslaved them, never worked out why they did it, or thought it was OK. It sounded cliched to her, but their thinking was so alien, so removed from what she knew was right and wrong, that she didn't even know where to start.

The doors slid shut behind them and a bead of sweat ran down her neck. The lift crept up to the higher decks, and hissed to a stop. They were all pressed back against the walls, as inconspicuous as possible, and her knuckles were white on the gun as the doors slid slowly open.

There was nothing, no one waiting, and the entire party seemed to relax together, shoulders dropping and hands unclenching. She sighed, and took a step out of the lift. Just ahead, a door in one side of the corridor opened, and four slaves stepped out. She had only a moment to realise that they wore the dark uniforms and carried guns before they opened fire. The second she got was enough to make her react, diving to the floor with a shout. The wave of gun fire hammered into the lift, deafening in the silence, and she covered her ears.

From behind her came return fire, smashing one of the slaves onto the floor and scattering the others. She yanked her gun up from her waist and fired, her first shots striking the ceiling. She closed an eye, trying to slow her breathing, and fired again, the bolt smashing into the face of a slave leaning against the wall. He slewed sideways, blood pouring from the wound, and she caught a glimpse of bone, sharp edges sticking out from his face. She shuddered, her stomach turning, then yelped as Lucid hurdled her and attacked the remaining slaves.

His blade was moving too fast for her to see, but she saw the slave nearest her reel back, blood spilling from a cut that went from his neck to his waist. He sank to the floor, hands trying to cover the long gash, blood welling between his fingers. Lucid moved past him and fought the final slave.

This one had time to prepare, and was frantically blocking the sword blows with his gun. Lucid seemed to move, without moving, sliding around the man, and brought his sword down, and she swallowed as a hand tumbled to the floor, bouncing in front of her. The man shrieked and dropped his gun, staggering backward as his left wrist sprayed blood. Lucid thrust his sword through the man's heart and he toppled to the floor.

The whole fight was over in seconds, and she lay where she was, breathing fast and trying not to look at the hand. She still couldn't get used to the fighting, to how quickly it all happened. She should have done something, used the spiritual to avoid all the bloodshed, but instead she'd just joined in, thoughtless and panic stricken.

Lucid calmly wiped his sword on the uniform of the dead man, as Stem and Atan reached her. They pulled her to her feet and they approached the slave still living, blood pouring from the wound. She was about to say something, some kind of apology, when Lucid stepped past and ran his sword through the man's eye. He slumped and she turned on the thin man, who stared back, one eyebrow raised, his mouth twisted up at the corner.

"Why did you do that?"

Even as she spoke, she realised how meaningless it was. It had to be done, and he had saved her the anguish. She should be thanking him, but it was just so cold, so matter of fact. He was still watching her, and she lowered the hand she had been waving at him, nodding slowly. He smiled, and patted her arm and she turned away. Life was becoming cheaper every second she spent out in the wide world.

The silence returned, more intense here where the throb of the engines was barely noticeable, and they stood for a moment, listening. Content they weren't about to be attacked, they followed Atan's directions to a room where Bridyant sat, clear plastic ties keeping her attached firmly to a chair fixed to the floor.

They rushed in, surrounding her and all talking at once in hushed voices. She smiled wanly, but Ally could see the huge bruise beginning to colour on the side of her face. Lucid sliced delicately through the bonds, and they helped her to stand, as which point she finally spoke.

"I'm alright, really, I'm OK, thank you. They hit me a few times, but nothing more."

She rolled her shoulders, glancing around the room.

"They also took my weapons."

Ally grinned. Her friend was far more worried about the loss of her sword and gun than the cuts and bruises she had suffered. Without another word, the alien disappeared into the next room, then emerged, bearing her weapons and a wide smile.

"Leaving your captive awake when you bring them in, very foolish."

She strapped them on.

"Thank you. This is very kind and very stupid of you, but I am grateful. We should leave now, yes?"

They ran out, back down the long corridor until they reached the lifts. Every step she expected to be stopped, for someone to emerge from a room and fire on them, or even worse, but much more likely, for the voice to begin, the Atrile themselves to speak, to close the net she felt surrounding her every second she was on board.

But they reached the lift safely, and when it opened at the bottom, the area was quiet. They walked quickly, resisting the urge to break into a run, as they headed back toward the hanger. The bay was empty, the docking bridge unattended and she shook her head, barely able to believe that it could be this easy. They jogged across the hanger and down the bridge, her heart lifting as she stepped back onto Gateway.

Without thinking about it, she let her mirror slip, and as she did, the voice crept in.

"Ahh, there you are. How curious, you seem to have just left our ship, now what would you be doing there?"

The others hadn't heard it, but they reacted to her face, the colour fleeing as she froze, then glanced quickly around. Still she could see nothing, but the voice came again.

"So sad that after the renegade slaves attack Gateway, another group decide to invade our ship. The captain will be intrigued to hear about it. He may have no choice but to put you out into space, alone... vulnerable."

The final word seemed to last for ever and she put one hand to her gun, running down the gantry. Wherever it was, it couldn't stop them getting back onto Gateway, and once they were there, she'd happily take her chances. She was huffing, sprinting as fast as she could, barely aware of the thumping boots of the others keeping up with her. She burst out of the gantry into the hall, and stopped, chest heaving.

It was the same as always, hundreds of travellers going about their business, a wall of noise and smell and colour that assailed her senses. Stem grabbed her arm, and pulled her around.

"What, what's up?"

"It spoke to me. It was a trap. I think it's convinced the captain that the humans who attacked us were runaways, not sent by the Atrile. It knew we were on the ship, it wanted us there, to prove to the Captain we broke the peace. It's blaming us for everything."

She spoke fast, eyes flicking around the room, searching. The others had crowded round and heard her words, and they joined her now, searching across the platforms for signs of the creatures. Suddenly, Lucid hissed, then pointed across the hall.

One of the Atrile was slowly descending the stairs, accompanied by a number of suited Gateway staff, Neve, and the captain. Even from here she could see him frowning, and she kicked the wall, balling her fists.

"Dammit, why would he believe them, he said he hated them?"

"This may well be an act, designed to get rid of them."

She looked at Atan, eyebrow raised, then shook her head.

"With the way things have gone for us lately, I doubt that very much."

She turned and watched, as they stepped onto the hall floor and were swallowed by the crowd. She had no intention of staying around to find out what the plan was, and began to walk, keeping calm, but moving as fast as she could, heading down the side of the hall. The others caught up, Atan jogging to keep up with her.

"Ally, is this really our best course of action? At the worst, he accuses us and we tell our side of the story. He can hardly deny the bruise Bridyant is sporting, can he? If we run off now, we look guilty."

"I'm not going to discuss anything with that creature. Sorry, but those things are evil, pure evil, and once it gets its claws in, people change, even when they think they can control it. We need to find a different way out of this."

"Which is?"

Lucid asked from her other side. She stopped, everyone else taking a step or two before turning back to her. She pointed at Stem.

"What he said. We find the controls for the weapons, and we blow the hell out of the Homeships."

She saw questions appear on everyone's faces, but this time, she didn't want to hide from them. It felt like the meeting they'd had, the first time they tried to kill the Lord. Everyone stared at her, expectant, as if she had all the answers. This time, she did, as simple as they were.

"This is a war. The Atrile need to be ended, and we swore to do it. I'm not going to bargain, or barter, or make out like we're open to negotiation. I want to kill them, all of them. We need to grab the advantage and hurt them, hurt them enough that they get scared, and question what they're doing."

She stopped talking, breathless and flushed. Lucid was the first to react, a wry smile spreading across his face.

"Despite your many flaws, I believe I am beginning to like you. I agree."

Stem was also nodding, the look he got when he was thinking about his parents on his face. She turned to Atan, who shook his head.

"There is a better way to do this, I am sure. But, I have promised to follow you, and help you, and for all my misgivings, that is what I shall do."

She grinned at him, and said "Splendid!"

He laughed, then motioned over her shoulder.

"How are we going to find the weapons' controls?"

Lucid smiled secretively, then motioned upward with his hands.

"I think I can take care of that. We need to get up a few levels though."

They ran for the nearest staircase, and scrambled up it. She glanced back to see the Atrile and his escort arrive at the gantry. They stopped, and turned to stare around the hall, and she ducked down, crouching as she took the steps. They'd just reached the platform, when a loud click rattled around the hall, followed by the tired-sounding voice of the captain.

"You are, I have no doubt, well aware that I would like to speak with you. Wherever you are, please come to the hall floor now."

They sprinted across the platform, all thoughts of caution thrown to the wind as they moved away from the open area. They found a set of escalators and charged up them, trying to remain unseen whilst pushing through the crowds. They came out on another platform, then they were brought to a dead stop by a wall of fire, roaring past them.

Ally shouted in alarm, then turned to see Neve fly in, her cannon aimed squarely at her. She jerked her head about, looking for an exit, but the only way up lay across the platform, across open ground. As before, the other travelers seemed equally scared, intrigued or bored. There would be no support from them. Neve stepped closer and Ally went to meet her.

"The captain has requested your presence."

"I know, but we can't. I'm sorry, but once we let the Atrile run things, we're screwed."

"That is between you and them, but my job is to take you down to the hall."

She raised the flame launcher, and Ally stepped back, hands in the air.

"Hey, OK, we're going, it's OK."

Neve nodded, then flew up and hovered, waiting. Ally stepped over to Stem, leaning against him and putting a hand around his waist. He read her and grabbed hold, taking the weight of her body as she slipped free. She hurtled across to the flying woman, and sunk inside. Her brain was alive and well, a multitude of fabulous colours, so strong in contrast to the slaves she had met. Neve knew she was there instantly, and tried to push her out, but Ally wrapped herself around her, strong against the pressure.

"Get out of my head!"

"I'm sorry, I'm so sorry, but I can't, not until you agree to leave us. Search elsewhere, say you couldn't find us, anything."

She tried to squeeze, to put more than just a request behind her words. It was easy, and she could feel Neve's mind changing, actually re-writing itself, and the pictures of her, and Stem and the others faded. She slipped out and watched as the woman took off and flew across the hall. She came back into her body, then staggered free of Stem's arms and vomited on the floor.

What she had just done was brainwashing, nothing less, and she felt dirty, and stained. They had forced this on her, driven her to it, and as she wiped the bile from the side of her mouth, she gritted her teeth, and turned to the others. They were staring at her, surprised, wide eyed. She glared at them, then walked past them to the stairs, and headed up.

Chapter 21

They found Feril a few platforms higher, hunched in a chair, sword and long dagger laid on the table before him. His eyes lit up when he saw them approach and he sprang to his feet. Lucid went to him, and they spoke quietly, in a language that sounded like a room full of people coughing. Then they turned as one to her, and Lucid cracked another smile. It was Feril who spoke.

"I knew it wouldn't be as they had said. Some things you just know, and must give allowances for those less-able of mind. You are looking for the weapons, I believe?"

She nodded, and he swept one arm out, indicating they should follow him. She was still for a moment, watching him walk away, and Lucid tapped her shoulder.

"You must trust somebody, sometime."

"I trust you."

"Then you can trust him. We are Larlien, and the bonds of our people lie far deeper than money or contract can bind."

Still she hesitated, and he nodded.

"Your caution is wise, but it may not be wisely placed. I am a thief, yet you trust me..."

She looked at him, and shrugged.

"And I don't know why."

He bowed, and patted his flat stomach lightly.

"Must be my natural charm and charisma."

She sighed, and took off after the security guard, who had reached the lifts and was now holding the doors.

They emerged onto the captain's level, but he led them away from the office, and around a corner into another section of the station. The room narrowed, curving until it became a corridor, still roofed with glass. From here, she could see a fraction of one of the Homeships, filling the view and blocking the stars.

The corridor continued to curve, and Feril bid them wait, continuing on alone. She heard him speak, then the hurried thumping of feet coming their way. Two security guards came rushing around the corner, and ran straight into them. Feril came behind, and smashed one over the back of the head at the same moment he froze and stared at them.

The other took another step, hand going to the communicator at his belt, before Bridyant leaped at him, and brought the butt of her gun crashing across his face. He dropped to the floor, and between them they dragged both guards back around the corner from where they'd come.

The corridor ended in a door, which slid open as Feril stood before it. He turned to them with a grin.

"These doors are set up to read people. There are only a few of us who have been given the pass."

The room that lay beyond was breathtaking. It felt like an enormous version of the Vale's cockpit, hundreds of banks of controls, and dials. In the centre was a massive chair, with sticks on both arms. Three quarters of the room was covered in windows, massive sheets of glass that stared out over the docking area. They spread out, exploring the room with wide-eyed amazement.

A thin layer of dust covered most of the surfaces. Bridyant ran a finger along the arm of the chair, lifting it off and showing Ally the dirt now attached to it. 'The station moves only rarely. So much beautiful technology, so underused.' She shook her head, and Ally grinned.

Lucid and Feril were examining one of the wall panels, flicking switches and muttering in hushed voices. Ally walked over to the window, putting her hands against the glass and staring out, past the sea of ships, to the great vastness that lay beyond. Atan came to stand next to her, looking first out into space, then at her.

"You are called, just as I am."

It wasn't a question, but she nodded anyway, and glanced at him.

"Yeah, I guess so. I haven't ever thought about, really. All we cared about was getting out, then getting to Earth."

She shook her head.

"It's weird, I've never even been there, but Earth already feels to small, you know?"

He smiled, nodding vigorously.

"This is how it feels, Ally, for explorers. We are not meant to be tied to a planet, to one place, but to the universe and all it contains."

He turned to the vista, spreading his arms wide. She imagined he would hold it in his hands if he could, sweep it into his warm embrace. When he turned back, his smile had fallen.

"Are you sure this is what you want to do? Violence is a dangerous destination, Ally, and one you might struggle to come back from."

She sighed, her breath frosting the glass. She didn't know what she wanted, except to stop running, to feel actually, truly, free.

"I don't know how else to do it. I don't know how to escape. And the slaves, Atan. They've wiped them clean. There aren't humans on those ships, just shells, walking and talking and pretending to be human. They'll never be free."

He watched her, silent, and when she turned to him, she felt tears prick her eyes.

"What else can I do?"

He opened his mouth, then closed it again, and shook his head.

"My people, when we began to dwindle, we shut ourselves away, hid from the universe. I couldn't agree with it, so I begged to be let go, and they let me, even against their misgivings."

He stopped, glancing back out of the window.

"The thought of being chained to my planet makes my heart shrivel, and my mouth go dry. Freedom, in our minds and hearts, is the undeniable truth of existence, yet you have lived the majority of your life without it."

He shook his head.

"I don't know what else you can do, and I cannot imagine truthfully how you must feel, but freedom must be fought for."

He turned and walked across the room, and she watched him go. She was startled by the speakers crackling into life, and the captain's voice booming through the room.

"We are now aware of your position, and of the damage you have caused on board the Homeship of our guests."

"They've got him, dammit, they've got him."

The others waved her to silence, listening to the rest of the address.

"There have been misunderstandings, I recognise that, so if we could get together and talk, please. This must be reconciled, if you are to remain on Gateway. Please come out now.'

He sounded reasonable, but she could hear the flatness in his voice, the lack of emotion that gave away the Atrile's deft touch. She walked straight over to where Lucid stood, and looked at the panel, where red lights now flashed and blinked.

"What do you think, can you make them work?"

He flashed her a smile, then indicated the panel.

"The system is warmed and your weapons are ready to fire."

She nodded tightly, and turned to the others. Bridyant had one hand on the central chair, watching her impassively, waiting. Atan was looking out the door and down the corridor, but he turned now to face her, nodding slightly. Stem was grinning, teeth and fists clenched, and she grinned back, feeling the butterflies begin. The two standing at the panel were equally eager, and she nodded. It was down to her, whether she liked it or not.

"What first?"

Lucid waved at the room.

"This room sits on the end of an arm, and can be turned. It is from here that the station is piloted. We turn this module until we can see our target."

Bridyant slung herself into the seat and grasped the sticks, moving them with her characteristic ease and calm. Ally watched for a moment, then the sound of running, boots thudding on metal, drew her attention away to where Atan was stood. His eyebrows were raised, and he waved a hand toward the centre seat.

"I think it would be wise to get moving now, please, Lucid."

Almost imperceptibly, the room began to move, and she dashed over to the doorway. Station staff were running toward them, and behind them, the Atrile, accompanied by the captain. It was staring into the room and when it saw her it began screaming, hands reaching out to her. She stepped back, the familiar chill running down her back, and put a hand on Atan's arm. The gap between the door and the corridor was narrowing as the module moved, and the Atrile sped up, its howling growing louder. She took another step back, wincing as the pain in her head grew more intense. She could see the sweat beading on the head of the nearest guard, his hands stretching out to the open gap. Then the door slid closed, and they vanished.

She gasped, relieved despite the piercing sound that still hammered at her brain, driving spikes deep in and making her stagger. She sat down, landing with a bump, and watched with blurry eyes as the four Homeships appeared before the window. Feril tapped furiously at the panel, and the sounds of pistons and machinery moving filled the module.

She closed her eyes, rubbing her temples at the incessant noise. She took another look around the room. It was amazing how much could change in such a short space of time. There were five other people in this room, people she trusted enough to contemplate entering the spiritual plane and leaving her unguarded body among them, not to mention leaving them to complete something she had started. There was something else as well, a warmth she suspected might last longer than this present moment.

The door controls beeped suddenly, making them all jump as the lights there went from yellow to flashing red, and the module shuddered to a stop. Feril rushed away from the panel, and across to the door. He hammered more keys, and the lights returned to yellow, the module moving again. He turned back to the room. 'We have not much time, the captain will have higher clearance than me.'

She lay down, a smile on her face, then drifted free of her body. Atan did the same and met her, floating in the middle of the room.

"This is a strange time to leave."

She shook her head.

"I'm not leaving, I just thought our friend outside might want to see what happens next."

She slid out the side of the module into space, then into the corridor, into the midst of the milling station staff. Two were clustered around the door controls, punching buttons. The captain looked frustrated, hovering behind them, and no doubt ready to jump in once their efforts were found to be useless. The Atrile was stock still, staring at the door, as if willing it to open. She sunk in, submerging herself in the strange wrongness, and laughed brightly as the screaming stopped.

The alien had a moment to realise what had happened before she grabbed it and yanked it free of its body, soaring up and through the roof of the corridor, dragging its spirit body with her. As they emerged into space, she threw it, sending it spinning away. It flew for a moment, then stopped and came hurtling back toward her, beak-like mouth open and snapping.

She put up a wall, and smiled again as it struck it, bouncing back then surging forward again, only to be thwarted again. She put her finger to her lips, and gestured where the Homeships hung around the giant gantry. It understood enough to turn and see where she was pointing, then it turned back, its glittering eyes telling her nothing.

"I thought you might like to see this, you and all your race. After we've finished here, we're heading to Earth."

She was about to continue, when a low-pitched whining began, making her entire spiritual body shake. Moments later, a blast of energy roared out from beneath the module and struck the nearest Homeship, tearing through the hull. Within seconds, the laser had cut through the ship and emerged from the other side. The beam then moved slowly upward, cutting the craft in two. The two halves parted, flames roaring up for a moment before being extinguished in the vacuum. Bodies floated out, the tiny, pathetic corpses of the humans whose brains had already died. She bit her lips, making herself watch, feeling the fire in her gut rise higher.

The Atrile that hung before her began to rant, howling at her, spitting and screaming threats. A whump that made her ears throb announced the arrival of rockets, a handful of steel capsules hurtling at the next Homeship. They struck at various points along the hull, and the entire side of the ship broke away, the insides exposed to space.

The creature's screaming got louder, and she winced, clapping her hands uselessly to her ears. She thought to strengthen the barrier, to block it out, but the pain was cutting through her attempts to concentrate. With a howl, she dropped the shield and threw herself at the creature.

She had only moments before they were locked together, the thing trying to push its claws inside her. For a second, she thought it would succeed, then the laser blasted again, striking another of the Homeships, and it reeled back, scream fading out.

She expanded her hands and wrapped them around its head. She squeezed, gritting her teeth. It screamed again, the pitch growing higher and higher as its head crumpled beneath her desperate hold. Then without warning, it vanished. She gasped, shaking, and turned back to watch the show. The two Homeships that had been hit were both wrecked, slewed over like wounded beasts, spilling liquids out into the blackness.

More lasers started up, huge beams wider than a gantry tearing through the remaining ships. She tried to find the revulsion Atan had been so worried about, but instead there was a pressure on her chest that made her shout, and punch the air, and kick with both legs. Less than a minute had passed and four Homeships had been destroyed, smoking hulks drifting slowly from the station and out into space. She only hoped they were occupied by the corpses of their owners.

She slid back into the corridor, where most of the station staff were dragging the dead body of the Atrile slowly back toward the captain's deck. The captain himself was standing, arms folded, watching the module with the faintest of smiles, hidden beneath a deep frown. She brushed past him and into the module, where the others were celebrating. She came back into her body and stood, then paced over to the window.

Stem came up to stand beside her, one hand pulling her close to him and she snuggled under his arm. In front of them, the four Homeships were disintegrating, dead chunks of metal, and she felt again that surge of energy in her that craved release. She twisted and threw her arms around Stem, kissing him soundly. Ally turned to the others, who greeted her with smiles.

Bridyant was quietly content, still sat in the chair, her hands wrapped around the sticks. Lucid muttered something to her and they both laughed. Only Atan looked less than joyful, his normally happy face stoic. She extricated herself from Stem's embrace and walked over to him.

"You still believe this was the wrong thing to do."

He rocked his head from side to side, and repeated the gesture with his flattened hands.

"I don't know. Something in me rebels against it, against the sheer destruction, but I see no other path, no other alternative."

He dropped his eyes, then looked back up at her, and his face split into a grin.

"But if I'm honest, I am once again impressed at what you've accomplished here. Well done, Ally. Our enemies on Earth should by now be somewhat scared, and that is no more than they deserve."

She clapped him on the shoulder, then started as the door slid open and the captain stepped through.

He glared at them, focusing on Ally until she quailed, then smiled sheepishly at him.

"Um, I hope you don't mind, we just borrowed Gateway for a moment."

He continued to stare and she looked at the others. Bridyant had one hand on her gun, and Lucid looked tense, and ready to spring into action. After what felt like an age, the captain's face broke into a grin, and he shook his head.

"That was a most rude and unreasonable way to act considering my hospitality, but once again, you have surprised me."

He spread his hands before him, and shrugged.

"No one can know that this was your doing and not mine. Gateway is my world, and under my control. Do you understand?"

She nodded emphatically. The captain walked over to the window, hands clasped behind his back, and stared out.

"The universe is changing. You started a fight when you escaped from the Atrile, but this is the beginning of the war. This is a declaration."

He shook his head, still staring out of the window, the rest of the room watching him. Finally he turned, looking somehow older to Ally, but he smiled at her.

"You are heading for Earth now?"

It was both a question and a nice way of telling them to leave, and she could finally accept it with good grace.

"Yeah, we'll go now."

She paused.

"Thank you."

He nodded, and strode from the room. She looked at the others, and followed the captain.

Outro

There was a certain sense of deja vu, only this time it wasn't just one ship leaving, but three. As the vast expanse of Gateway dwindled in the rear screens, she found herself drifting back. She had thought about the past more in the last few weeks than ever before in her life.

Dad kept appearing in her mind, his face, the way he'd taught her stuff, the sound of his voice. He wouldn't have believed everything that had happened since that last game, but he'd have been proud of her, she was sure of that.

She glanced at Atan and Lucid, sat in the bunk room, talking animatedly, sharing their many years of experience. They talked of a universe she was only just beginning to explore. They were heading for Earth, there to fight a war that could change the universe, change the way people thought. It was terrifying, but it felt like the right kind of fear.

After that? That was a question she was scared of answering. She looked over at Stem, then back at

the screens. It was a question that could wait. Today, they were heading for Earth.

Thank You

Thanks for reading
A Game of War Season Two.
If you have enjoyed what you've read,
please leave a review at
amazon.com/author/michaelcairns

Sign up for the newsletter for
information on future releases and
free short stories at:
http://cairnswrites.com/sign-up

Connect with me online:
http://twitter.com/cairnswrites
http://goodreads.com/michaelcairns
http://facebook.com/cairnswrites
http://pinterest.com/michaelcairns

Acknowledgements

The print version of this book has taken a long time. A looooong time. Mostly, I've been focused on writing more books and releasing them. But also it's because life, as it so often does, has just got in the way.

Having two young children, three careers and a healthy chocolate addiction to feed leaves me precious little time for the important things in life, like print formatting and eating chocolate.

Anyway, thanks must go to my wonderful wife for her constant and unrelenting encouragement and support. To my mum and dad for the same, as well as pre-cooked meals, advent calendars and a never ending supply of good café recommendations.

Thanks to Mark and the lovely people at Kobo for putting Childhood Dreams on a special page and helping people find it. Also, just for being lovely and really interested in authors. Very cool people.

Finally, as per usual, thanks to you, the reader, for staying with me and picking up the print copies that, despite how wonderful my ereader might be, are still the most exciting part of this whole crazy writing journey.

Also available from Michael Cairns:

Thirteen Roses, the series: A Paranormal Zombie
Saga

One - Before
Two - After
Three - Beyond
Four - Alone
Five - Home
Six - Despair
Seven - War

Assassin's Song: A Dark Fantasy Trilogy

Assassin's Lament
Assassin's Chant
Assassin's Aria

Ninja Zombie Killers: A Comedy Horror, Rock
and Roll Odyssey

Books I - IV available now

The Planets: A Science Fiction Superhero Series

The Spirit Room
The Story of Eris
The Long Way Home

Forgotten Dreams: A Collection of Science Fiction, Fantasy, Superhero, Paranormal and Speculative Fiction short stories

A Spider Dreams: 15 Creepy Short Stories of Horror, Mayhem and Children's Birthday Parties

ABOUT THE AUTHOR

Michael Cairns is the author of over 20 novels and 70 short stories spread across an unhealthily wide range of genres, including, but not limited to, Fantasy, Horror, Science Fiction, Zombie, Paranormal, and Comedy.

He has two children, one wife, a house in Buckinghamshire and not enough snare drums. Also, he likes chocolate.

www.ingramcontent.com/pod-product-compliance
Lightning Source LLC
Chambersburg PA
CBHW021953170626
46808CB00001B/140